HIS HIDDEN STAR

AN AGE-GAP, FRIENDS-TO-LOVERS, SMALL TOWN
INSTA-LOVE ROMANCE

HIDEAWAY VALLEY FIRE
BOOK ONE

ELIZA ROCKWOOD

©2024 by Eliza Rockwood

All rights reserved.

No part of this book may be reproduced in any form or by any electronic or mechanical means, including information storage and retrieval systems, without written permission from the author, except for the use of brief quotations in a book review.

This story is a work of fiction. Names, characters, places, and incidents are the product of the author's imagination or are used fictitiously. Any resemblances to actual events, locales, or persona, living or dead, is coincidental.

Cover: © 2024 by Thomas Ward.

❦ Created with Vellum

To my readers—thank you for taking a chance on my books, and making the dreams of a shy, anxious little girl come true. I grew up using the stories in my head as a way to escape the realities of an unstable home, and as I got older, I started putting those fantasies down on paper. Love stories have always been my greatest comfort —a warm, safe retreat from reality. I hope my books can be that for you; that you can see pieces of yourself in my characters, and feel less alone in this big, crazy world.

READER CONTENT NOTES

This book contains the following:

- Adult themes and language, including fully described sex scenes with dirty talk
- Memories of non-consensual and traumatic past sexual experiences (not between main characters)
- Stalking of a main character by a side character, and references to mental illness

ABOUT

Ashlyn

I've devoted the last decade of my life to acting. I've given up friends, family, romance—absolutely *everything* to pursue my career—hoping that one day I'll finally live up to my father's legacy. Instead, I'm snubbed at the Oscars and quickly become the laughingstock of Hollywood. The passion I once felt for being on the big screen begins to fade away, and for the first time since I started out in Hollywood, I find myself longing for time away from the spotlight.

So, I decide to retreat to the mountain town I visited a year ago, and reconnect with the one man I can't seem to forget. Will I finally be able to let my guard down, and allow Chase to heal my fractured heart?

Chase

The moment I met Ashlyn, I knew I'd met *the one*. But she's a world-famous actress and I'm just a small-town fire chief—not to mention I'm over a decade older than her. No matter how much I may want it, what hope could I possibly have at winning her love?

To my surprise, Ashlyn stayed in touch after meeting me a year ago, and now she's back in Hideaway Mountain. She arrives in town a broken woman, who needs someone to take care of her—to put her first and love her the way she's always deserved—and I'm more than ready for the job. It's time to finally make Ashlyn *mine*—once and for all.

ASHLYN

When my ex first told me he was done with Hollywood, I must admit—I was incredulous. I couldn't understand why he'd leave a successful acting career for a tiny Colorado town, practically in the middle of nowhere.

After yet another year on location though, I'm starting to understand his reasoning. I've been making movies for over a decade, never slowing down, never taking time to consider if being on screen still makes me happy. Not only am I exhausted from the constant work, but my passion for being in front of a camera isn't the same as it used to be.

Lately, I've been feeling like something is missing.

I guess maybe it's starting to show in my work too. When the Oscar nominations were announced I was snubbed, even though I'd won a Golden Globe and everyone seemed to think I was a shoo-in for a nomination. The Academy clearly thought differently, and now, as a result, I've become the laughingstock of Hollywood.

Running away to the mountains sounds like a perfect solution.

My ex, Will, escaped to the tiny town of Hideaway Mountain following our public breakup, which painted him in a terrible light across the media.

Will and my relationship had never been much more than a friendship, and a convenient way to help our careers by creating positive press around our *"love story."*

I was on location in the U.K. when my sleazy director kissed me, which the paparazzi conveniently captured on camera, proclaiming I'd found a *"new love."* My now former publicist decided to use the picture and tabloid speculation about our relationship as a way to promote my new film, and released a statement that we'd broken up.

We *hadn't,* at least not formally, but the news got to Will before I could.

Thinking I'd cheated and dumped him, Will left L.A., also changing all his contact information before I could talk to him. Eventually, after begging his agent for information, I managed to track him down.

I went to Hideaway Mountain to apologize and make sure he was okay, inadvertently almost ruining his burgeoning relationship with the local inn owner. Luckily, we were able to convenience Will's now wife, Flora, that I wasn't there to try and win him back, and that we'd never been in love in the first place.

Now, almost a year later, Will and Flora are happily married with a new baby. If asked, Will would tell you that our break up and media scandal was the best thing that ever happened to him. Because of it, he left Hollywood and met the love of his life. It was also the push he needed to start work on screenwriting, his real passion, which is now blossoming into a successful career.

Will obviously made the right decision to leave California when he did, and I'm finally starting to understand why he took that leap of faith into the unknown.

When your life starts to implode around you, there's nothing left to do but jump.

Will and I have stayed friends, and since I know he understands what I'm going through better than anyone, today I decided to reach out and ask for his advice.

Flora had already texted me this morning in our group chat after yet another terrible meme of me on social media started to go viral. We've become close too, I don't have many real friends, and she wanted to make sure I was okay. So, it wasn't a surprise when I called.

I ended up Facetiming with them both, telling them I was thinking about a long-term getaway to Colorado, especially considering how good it ended up being for Will. I asked if they thought I was crazy for wanting to take a break, despite still being one of the most sought-after actresses in Hollywood. They told me they'd be thrilled to have me in town, and Flora especially encouraged me to follow my heart.

And my heart has been telling me to go back. I long for the peace and beauty of the town, and to spend time with Will, Flora, and their new baby boy, but those aren't the only reasons Hideaway Mountain calls to me.

There is a *much* bigger reason, and his name is Chase Morath—the firefighter I met during my first visit to Hideaway.

A man I've not been able to get my mind off since.

Sometimes I think he might be *exactly* what's missing in my life.

Chase and I exchanged contact information after meeting, and though he recognized my face from being plastered all over the media, he wasn't too familiar with my work.

In true mountain man fashion, Chase doesn't pay much attention to entertainment news or watch many movies (at least, he didn't before he met me). I thought for sure without my star power he'd forget all about me after I left, but I was wrong.

He texted me almost immediately to check I'd made it home safe, and we've kept in touch ever since. Hardly a day goes by that we don't talk in one form or another.

We've become great friends.

So, after talking to Will and Flora, I begin texting him right away. I want to be sure he also won't mind me visiting the place he calls home.

Before I can hit send though, Chase beats me to the punch.

This type of thing happens *all the time*. If I didn't know better, I'd think we have some sort of strange, telepathic connection.

> Hey princess, how are you today? Hope you're not letting all that bullshit online get you down.

Chase started calling me princess after he watched a fantasy movie I starred in, where I played the spirited daughter of a king. After meeting me, he decided to start catching up on all my films. The nickname started as Princess Amara (my name in the movie), but quickly devolved to just *princess*.

I never thought I'd enjoy being called something like that, especially considering a lot of people who don't know me think I'm a stuck-up, spoiled brat. But coming from Chase—I *love* it.

When he calls me princess, it makes me feel cared for. Even *precious*.

I've never been precious to anyone before.

Since we talk almost every day, Chase knows how upset I've been since the Oscar news. But the meme going viral today has been the worst yet.

It depicts my frowning father, looking down on me in disappointment from heavenly clouds with the quote: *"She might be Hollywood royalty, but even Dad knows you can't inherit talent."*

My father was an incredibly famous and well-respected director. My family has been working in the industry since the early days of film.

The Addison's are a legacy in Hollywood.

I was the first to venture into acting, and though my dad and I weren't exactly close, I always wanted to make him proud.

He'd be so ashamed if he could see me now…

I pause before texting Chase back, smiling that he thought to check in on me, probably after seeing that nasty meme.

It makes me wonder, like I have many times, if maybe… *just maybe*…Chase sees me as more than a friend.

I shake the notion off though, like always.

Chase is older and drop-dead gorgeous, towering over anyone else in a room and built like a tank—with thick, almost black hair dusted with bits of gray, and deep, ocean-colored eyes. The man could've been a model. Many of the actors I work with are considered some of the best-looking men in the world, but none of them compare to Chase.

I don't know if Hideaway Valley does firefighter calendars, but if they do, Chase should be on every page.

Shirtless.

They'd sell out in a heartbeat.

I've never seen him like that, half-naked, but I've certainly thought about it a lot.

And Chase isn't just a firefighter; he's the chief. Hideaway Valley is small in population, but since the district covers a lot of land prone to wildfire, his role is a huge responsibility. Chase is a respected pillar of his community and probably has his pick of the women in town and the tourists who travel through.

Sure, I'm a famous actress who many consider to be beautiful, but what am I beyond that, *really?*

Chase has *depth.* He's smart and funny and saves lives for a living. I just memorize lines and look pretty on screen. He probably considers me like a little sister, much as he does Flora. She's always referred to him as the brother she never had.

So no, Chase doesn't see me like *that,* even if I wish he did. I should quit pining and be glad he's in my life at all.

He's the best friend I have, and I don't want to do anything to jeopardize our relationship.

With that thought in mind, I text him back.

> Hey! Thanks for checking on me. You must have seen that awful meme.

> Yeah. I hope you don't take that crap too seriously. Whoever made that doesn't know the real you. I'm sure your dad would be proud of you.

I can't help but snort out a laugh.

> Thanks, but you didn't know my dad. It's okay though, I'm trying to ignore it. Maybe I'll throw my phone and laptop out the window so I can't see any of it anymore, lol

> Don't do that princess. Then how would we talk?

I smile at my phone. Even if Chase doesn't want me the way I want him, I know he definitely *likes* me and values our friendship.

I decide to use his question as my opening to tell him my plan to come to Hideaway.

> Actually, we might be able to talk in person soon. I'm thinking about taking a little break from everything and coming back to Hideaway.

Don't tease me, Ashlyn. Really?

> Lol yes, really! If I come, will you hang out with me?

Of course I will. Do you have any idea how much I want to see you again, in person?

I beam as I text him back, brimming with excitement. *This was a great idea*, I think.
I've not felt this happy or this at peace in *weeks*.
Maybe ever.

> It's settled then! I'll start getting everything set up. Hopefully, I can leave in a few days. Are you sure my being there won't cramp your style?

I don't want Chase to give up anything just because I'm around. I don't know much about his day-to-day life outside work, which is what he talks about most often. Surely though, working can't be *all* a man like him does. Chase probably goes out in town to places my fame will likely keep me from enjoying—even in a tiny place like Hideaway.

Maybe he goes out on a lot of dates.

I shudder at the thought.

> What style? Princess, all I do is work, grab the occasional beer and bite at the inn, and talk to you.

I'm glad we're only texting, so Chase can't see me blush. I can't possibly be that important to him.

Can I?

> Okay, if you're sure. I'll let you know when I get everything set.

> Good. I've got a lot of unused vacation, so I'll take some time off too. If you're sure you really want to hang out with an old, grumpy fire chief.

I giggle. He's always saying stuff like that, even though I tell him all the time that he isn't *old*. After a lot of prodding, I got him to admit that he's 42, though based on his self-deprecation you'd think he was in his 60's. I'm 28, so it's not like he's *that* much older than me.

> For the millionth time, you're not old! And there is nothing I'd like more than to hang out with you, Chase.

> Good. Let me know once your plans are set.

> Will do. Can't wait to see you!

> ;-)

Oh my god, I think. *Did he just send me an emoji— a winking emoji?*

The man has never, in all of our conversations, ever used one. Did he mean to do that? And if so, why the wink?

What does that *mean*?

Before I can overanalyze the situation, I distract myself by making travel plans.

I know most other people with my status and wealth would use an assistant for this type of thing, but I prefer to do things for myself. It's the same reason I didn't try and get my dad to help me in the film industry. He gave me some money for an agent, and I know my name got me auditions, but I did the rest of it myself. It was *my* talent that got me my first roles.

If not always just my *acting* talent.

I clear that thought with a shake of my head—not a rabbit hole I want to let myself go down.

Instead, I arrange for my private jet and book a house to stay at that's about halfway between the towns of Hideaway Mountain and No Name Creek. It's gated for security and surrounded by land with no neighbors for miles.

With that all taken care of, I text Chase, Will, and Flora to let them know I'll be in town the day after tomorrow.

Soon I'll be out of Hollywood.

Soon I'll be far enough away that maybe I can forget all about the Oscars and the tabloids and the memes...and the one other thing that makes me want to get out of town.

The thing I've not told anyone about, other than my bodyguard.

For the past few months, I've been getting creepy letters, dead flowers, and other...*odd* gifts outside the gate of my home or left on the hood of my car. I hired a driver because of it, so my car is never left unattended, and my bodyguard, Beau, started staking out my house and even put up more cameras. But whoever my stalker is, he's never shown up as much more than a shadow on the security footage.

The letters proclaim his undying love, that we're *"meant to* be together," and that he's *"always watching"* me. He signs them as *"Eternally Yours."*

Creepy. As. Hell.

I reported it to the police but there isn't much they can do, especially as he hasn't threatened me and we have no idea who he is. Stalkers are, after all, common for celebrities. My only recourse has been to have either Beau or another guard on his team stay at my home and travel with me 24-7 just so I can feel safe.

I suppose I should have mentioned it to Chase, Flora, or Will, but I didn't want to worry them. Especially since I'm probably overreacting anyway. This *"Eternally Yours"* isn't the first stalker I've had, and I've never been too worried about it before.

Something about this stalker *does* feel different, though.

The things this guy says and the gifts he leaves make my skin crawl.

I shake myself, clearing my mind of my stalker and the other not-so-pleasant reasons I'm leaving town, and focus on the good ones instead.

I'm finally going back to Hideaway.

I get to see and hopefully *touch* Chase again—even if it's only a hug.

As I finalize my plans and start to pack, I find myself fantasizing about Chase, recalling the way it felt to be wrapped in his strong arms when he told me goodbye, and the press of his big, hard body against mine.

I felt so protected and so cherished when I was with him. Chase is bigger than any bodyguard I've ever had, but it's not just his size that makes me feel so secure. It's also the look in his navy-colored eyes whenever they find and focus on mine; like if I asked him to, he'd lasso me the moon—just like Jimmy Stewart in *It's a Wonderful Life.*

And it's the way his broad shoulders soften and relax

whenever he sees me, his solemn face unwinding, and his full lips twitching up into a smile.

I'd do almost anything to see Chase smile.

And I'd *kill* to get his lips on mine—to have him kiss every inch of my body.

I know it will never happen, but a girl can dream.

Right?

CHASE

Ashlyn will be here any minute, I think as I wipe my sweaty palms down the front of my T-shirt.

I sure am a nervous wreck for a man whose entire job is to remain calm in high-pressure situations. As the chief of the Hideaway Valley Fire District, I'm usually stoic and unflappable, even when responding to the most horrific car accidents or intense wildfires. But when it comes to Ashlyn, I'm a mess.

Always have been.

Ever since the first time I saw her, walking into the pub at the Hideaway Inn with her ex-boyfriend Will, I've been completely gone for the girl. I don't watch much TV or many movies, but I recognized her right away as someone I'd seen on the cover of magazines. I couldn't place her name immediately, but from the start, I knew she was famous and way out of my league.

But try telling that to my poor, wasted heart.

I'm completely and hopelessly in love with her.

It's ridiculous—I know. Ashlyn Addison, one of the most

beautiful women in the world, an international superstar actress, would never want me the way I want her.

And yet I continue to hang on, some delusional part of my brain unwilling to accept that Ashlyn only sees me as a friend—a *much* older brother (I'm not old enough to be her father, thank god, unless I'd been an extremely promiscuous middle schooler).

I'm lucky to be in her life at all, considering I acted like a complete fool right after we met. I was bossy and possessive with her, as though I had some sort of claim to stake. I'd wanted to throw her over my shoulder and carry her away like a caveman.

I still can't believe she gave me her number before she left town, and I was even more shocked when she responded to my first text. After that, we started talking regularly.

Hardly a day passes that we don't. Even when she was in a different time zone overseas on location, I'd sacrifice sleep to see her for a few minutes on Facetime.

As famous as Ashlyn is, she doesn't have many real friends or people who treat her like a normal human being. I think that's what she must like about me, and why she's let me into her world.

She's a lonely woman looking for genuine friends.

And when it comes to Ashlyn, I'll take anything I can get.

When she told me she was coming back to Hideaway, I was more than a little surprised. I knew she'd been down since losing the Oscar nomination, and because of all the cruel videos and memes people have been putting up about her. I never thought she'd willingly take a break from her career though.

Since meeting Ashlyn, I've watched most of her movies (except the one with her ex, Will, since I can't stomach seeing them together), and her passion for her work is apparent in all her films.

I never thought she'd want to give that up, even temporarily.

Just like I never thought I'd want to take a vacation from the fire district. I've been working as a firefighter and paramedic since I moved to Hideaway Valley over two decades ago and can count the number of days off I've taken on one hand.

My job has been my whole life for *years*. Every meaningful relationship I have is a result of it; my district team is the closest thing I have to a family.

My dad passed away shortly after my move to the mountains, and my mom is still alive but lives in a care home in Denver. Thanks to her dementia, she no longer knows who I am.

The only other significant person in my life is Flora, who became like a little sister to me after I saved her life when she was only three. Flora now owns the local Hideaway Inn and is married to Will.

Duty has always come first for me, so there's never been time for anyone else in my life. When I started as a paramedic, I vowed that I'd spend the rest of my life honoring the name of my father—my guilt for failing him driving me to live only for work. Love used to be the farthest thing from my mind, and even sex always came secondary to my job.

I used to occasionally go to one of the bars in No Name Creek and pick up a tourist for a one-night stand or a week-long hook-up, but once I took over as chief those trips became less and less frequent, eventually drying up completely. Not only was I too busy to spend the time trying to find a willing partner, but the lack of connection that came with meaningless sex always left me feeling hollow.

I've been abstinent by choice for years, and I don't see that changing anytime soon. Ashlyn's the only one I want, and sex or no sex, she's the only woman I'll ever let into my heart. I'd do *anything* for my princess—even if she isn't really mine.

So, when Ashlyn said she was coming to town, I didn't hesitate for a second to put in for my vacation. Javier, my second in command, laughed when I first told him he'd be taking over for a few weeks, thinking I must be joking. But as soon as I told him *why* I'd be stepping away, he knew I was serious.

Everyone seems to know how gone I am for Ashlyn, even if the girl herself is completely unaware.

I'm so far gone that I offered to come and check in for her at the place she rented, to make sure everything was ready and to double-check security.

Ashlyn's bodyguard is traveling with her and staying for one night before taking a long overdue vacation of his own. Beau will also thoroughly check security, but I want to see for myself that everything is top-tier.

I won't be able to sleep unless I'm certain Ashlyn is safe.

I arrived at the mini-mansion she rented a couple of hours ago. The property manager is a guy I've seen around, and he must know who I am too as he was puzzled to find me here checking in for his guest.

Ashlyn used a fake name, of course, so he kept prying for more information—probably wondering how someone like me could be connected with the person renting this ridiculously expensive house.

What he doesn't know is despite her wealth and fame, Ashlyn is a simple woman with simple tastes. The only reason she picked this huge place is because she needs the security of fully-monitored and gated grounds. No one other than Beau knows she's staying here, but you can never be too safe.

When the property manager couldn't take a hint to stop with all the questions, I finally gave the little man a stern look and told him it was none of his business, which shut him up fast. I'm a big guy at over 6'8", and what little time I spend outside of work I spend training, so I'm the last man most people want to fuck with.

Eventually, I got him to leave, feeling like a dick for being so intimidating but also not wanting to risk Ashley's privacy. Then I checked the place from top to bottom; not just for security but for her comfort, ensuring there were plenty of clean towels, that the AC was set not too hot or too cold, and ensuring the kitchen was stocked with good coffee.

I know how my princess needs her caffeine.

Now, after all that, I'm anxiously waiting on the front porch, ready to hit the button on the remote in my hand to open the gate as soon as she arrives.

I'm like a fucking golden retriever waiting for his master to get home.

It's pathetic, but I can't bring myself to care.

Ashlyn Addison owns me. Heart and soul.

And I'd love nothing more than for her to own my body too...

I'm losing myself in thoughts of Ashlyn— her dark auburn hair and pretty hazel eyes, her softly curved body spread out below me, pressing against my chest and hands as I explore every inch of her—when I hear a car approaching.

Rocks crunch under its wheels as it gets closer, and my phone buzzes in my pocket, pulling me from my daydream.

> I'm here!

I grin as I open the gate, and watch as the black SUV approaches and parks. Before I can so much as blink, Ashlyn is flying out of the car and crashing into my arms.

Her hands grab the back of my neck as she flies at me, her long legs wrapping around my waist.

I'm so shocked it takes me a second to hug her back.

This feels more like a greeting for a lover than a friend.

But that can't be right. She can't *really* mean it that way.

Can she?

"Chase," she whispers in my ear. "I'm so happy to see you. I missed you so much."

My hands are sliding from where they grip her waist dangerously close to her ass. I'm getting ready to pull back just enough so I can see her face, try to make sense of this moment, and maybe even try for a kiss, when the clearing of a throat behind us breaks the spell.

Instead of slowly lowering Ashlyn down, and allowing her to feel *exactly* what she does to me, I drop her like a hot potato—suddenly certain she'd be disgusted if she felt my body's reaction to having her so close.

She makes a disappointed sound as her feet touch the ground, but before I can apologize or question my actions, her bodyguard speaks up from behind us.

"Hey Chase," he says, approaching me with his hand out, and I reach to shake it. "Good to see you again."

Beau was with Ashlyn on her trip when we first met a year ago, since my girl is smart enough to know that someone with her status isn't safe without security.

He's a big guy too, though not as big as me, with dark hair and matching eyes. He's wearing his usual attire of all black, and I suppose he'd be considered handsome by most.

When we'd first met, I felt a stab of jealousy, knowing it's not uncommon for men in his position to end up with the women they protect. But as soon as I talked to Beau, I realized he's all business. Still, I'm glad he won't be staying for Ashlyn's trip, because *I* want to be the one who protects her.

I'll be taking over the role of bodyguard for the next few weeks—a thought that brings a smile to my lips and a twitch to my neglected cock.

I internally shake myself, pulling my brain out of the gutter where it's quickly going again, and force my focus on the man standing in front of me.

"Good to see you too, Beau," I reply, shaking his hand once before letting it drop. "I've checked the place from top to bottom, and all seems to be in order. I'm sure you'll still want to do your own checks though. You're the expert, after all."

Beau nods, his eyes narrowing as he starts to scan the layout of the house and surrounding grounds.

"Yeah, and I'll be adding a few additional cameras as well, just in case. I'll give you access to everything too, since you'll be filling in for me with Miss Addison the next few weeks."

I nod, fighting a smile. Not only am I pleased that I'll be taking care of Ashlyn while she's here, but I also always appreciate how professional Beau is with her. He's been her bodyguard for a couple of years, and yet still keeps things formal—even though I know she's told him over and over to call her Ashlyn.

"Thank you again for dropping everything for me, Chase. I'm so grateful to be here with you," Ashlyn beams up at me, taking my arm with her delicate hand and squeezing my bicep as she speaks. "And I know Beau is grateful too, even if he won't say so out loud. Do you know this is the first vacation he's taken the entire time he's worked for me?"

Beau just grunts as he continues his survey and pulls out his phone, snapping a few pictures. He's a man of few words and devoted to his work, much like me.

"If you want to help Miss Addison with her things, I can get started on checking security and installing the cameras," Beau says, already turning towards the door to the house.

Ashlyn leads me to the SUV and pops open the back to start pulling out her things. I'm surprised when I only see one suitcase and a small duffle. She's planning to be here for at least three weeks, so I would have figured she'd pack more.

"This is it?" I ask, easily pulling out her suitcase and slinging her bag over my shoulder.

"Yup," Ashlyn says. "I figured I could always buy anything I may have forgotten. You know I'm low maintenance, Chase," she teases, and I smile in response.

If you believed all the shit written about her, you'd think Ashlyn was a stuck-up ice queen, who wouldn't travel without a hoard of servants and an entire wardrobe of bags. But that's not who my princess is.

Ashlyn is sweet-natured and reserved, quiet and introspective.

Once I've got everything from the car, Ashlyn tucks her arm back through mine as we walk towards the house, almost like she can't stop touching me.

I won't complain about that.

I lead Ashlyn through the entryway and up the stairs to the primary suite, and she comments on the amazing views as we pass the many windows.

The house she picked is situated firmly in the valley between the towns of No Name Creek and Hideaway Mountain, so the rocky land slopes up on both sides, dotted with spruce, aspen, and the red poppies of late summer. It's September, and I know Ashlyn is excited to see the fall colors as they gradually paint the landscape over the next few weeks.

I'm glad she selected the place she did, as it's only about a 10-minute drive from my cabin outside of No Name Creek. That way if she needs me, or there's an emergency, I'll be able to get here quickly. The emergency services in the area have a great response time too, but I still like knowing that she's nearby.

Even if I'd *rather* she be in my house, with me.

Preferably in my bed.

Oh well, you can't always get what you want, I think to myself.

I'm just glad she's here, closer than I ever thought she'd be again.

I'm telling myself to be grateful for that as I lead her to the bedroom, placing her suitcase near a dresser and her bag on the large king-sized bed.

"This is so nice," Ashlyn remarks, taking in the space. "This bed is huge though," she sounds disappointed, and I frown with concern.

"You don't like that?" I ask. I figure most people prefer a big bed to a small one.

"No, it's fine," she answers. "It's just…I always feel so *alone* in beds this big…" Her eyes dart to mine, and they look sad and almost…*pleading.*

I know Ashlyn is often lonely, but she can't possibly want me to stay with her in this bed.

Right?

I'm frozen, not sure what to say, and I must take too long because Ashlyn wipes her face of emotion and looks away, forcing a smile.

Shit. I think.

I feel like I keep disappointing Ashlyn. Saying the wrong thing, or more likely, saying nothing at all—searching my mind and failing to find the right words.

"Anyway," Ashlyn switches gears, her tone brightening. "I'm going to clean up out of this," she gestures down at the yoga pants and loose-fitting shirt she's wearing, chestnut hair pulled into a messy bun. "And then Flora and Will invited us over for dinner if that sounds good?"

I nod, trying not to show the uncomfortable feeling her words elicit.

It's not that I don't want to go to Flora and Will's for dinner. I like Will, Flora is practically family, and they have a brand-new baby I'm looking forward to seeing again. But I still can't seem to help the jealousy that starts to simmer inside me, knowing Will and Ashlyn were together once—for nearly a *year*.

I know they never loved each other. Their so-called romance was based on friendship and being together publicly benefitted their careers, but that doesn't change the fact that they *were* together.

It doesn't seem to bother Flora though, as she and Ashlyn have become good friends, and I know Will's entire world orbits around Flora and little Liam.

So, I need to get over it.

I know they're Ashlyn's only other true friends and a big part of the reason she came back to town. I have no intention of standing in the way of that. But it doesn't mean it won't make me slightly crazy.

Ashlyn is *mine. My princess.*

The thought floats through my head unbidden, and I force it away.

If I keep letting my lizard brain think for me and act like a possessive fool, I'm going to push Ashlyn away.

Which is the last thing I want.

"Sounds good, princess," I answer. "I'll just wait downstairs until you're ready."

"Great," Ashlyn says. As I turn to leave her to it, she grabs my wrist, pulling me gently back.

"I can't tell you enough how glad I am to be here Chase," she squeezes my hand, and that longing look is back in her pretty green-brown eyes.

Ashlyn is so close that I can smell her cherry blossom scent, and see the swell of her round, perky breasts; the outline of her nipples visible as they push against the fabric of her shirt with each breath. "I know we talk all the time, but it's just not the same. I *missed* you. So much."

"I know princess," I reply, squeezing her hand as I turn towards the door. I need to get out of here—put some distance between us before I do something we'll both regret.

"I feel exactly the same way."

ABOUT TWENTY MINUTES later we arrive at Will and Flora's place in Hideaway Mountain, a stone's throw from the inn Flora used to run and still owns. Her cousin Callum took over managing the place after she got married, and the home she built with Will sits on the nearby land that's been in her family for generations.

It's large, but not obnoxiously so, built to blend into the scenery of the mountainside and nearby river. There's a large wrap-around porch, and the home has more windows than walls. It's fitting for Flora, who now works in conservation and loves the outdoors.

Flora and Will are standing outside to greet us when we arrive, and Will has his newborn son strapped to his front, cradled in his arms. Little Liam is only a few weeks old, his shock of dark red hair, inherited from his mother, peeking out from behind the strap securing him to his father.

The new parents both look tired, but also blissfully happy, and I can't help the pang of jealousy that flows through me.

I want what they have.

And I want it with Ashlyn.

Before I can dwell too much on my spiraling thoughts, Ashlyn rushes over to hug Flora and then Will—slightly awkwardly to keep from crushing Liam, and then begins cooing over the little boy as I greet his parents.

That yearning look is back on Ashlyn's pretty face, and when she glances at me while stroking Liam's tiny head, I swear I see my own desires reflected in her eyes.

Could she want a family too, with *me?*

Is that truly possible?

"Thank you both so much for having us over," Ashlyn says as she continues stroking Liam's round cheeks. He gurgles in response. "I hope it's not too much trouble, especially since you have your hands so full now."

"It's no trouble at all," Flora says, smiling at Ashlyn and then down at her son from where she stands at Will's side. "We've been going a little stir-crazy since Liam arrived, so it's nice to have people over. I'll admit we did pick up most of the food from the inn though. One of these days we'll get back to cooking, once we're getting a bit more sleep at night."

"Can we help with anything?" I ask.

"Sure," Flora answers. "How about you help me bring all the food out to the table on the back patio? It's such a nice evening, we thought we could eat outside. While we do that, Will can give Ashlyn the tour, since it's her first time here."

I nod, even though I don't like the idea of Ashlyn and Will being alone together. It's ridiculous, I know, but my stupid caveman brain doesn't seem to listen to logic.

"That sounds great!" Ashlyn exclaims excitedly. "I'd love to see it all. It's so beautiful from the outside."

"Let's go then," Will says, leading us all inside. He takes Ashlyn up a set of stairs near the entryway, while I follow Flora back into their kitchen. As soon as we arrive, I realize why Flora sent Will off to show Ashlyn around.

She knows how I feel about Ashlyn, even if I've never outwardly admitted it, and she wants to grill me. It's written all over her smirking face.

I groan internally.

"So," Flora starts as she gathers utensils and pulls food

and drinks out from a large refrigerator, placing them on the island in the center of the room. "You must be pretty happy to have Ashlyn in town?"

I'm still gritting my teeth at the thought of her walking around the house alone with Will, but I nod. "I am."

"Really? Because you look pissed about it," Flora teases. I'm sure my face looks like thunder at the moment, but I've always been a bit of a grump. Flora's known me most of her life though, so she's used to it.

"I figured you'd be smiling from ear to ear when you got here with her. But right now, you look like you want to punch something, Chase."

I sigh. I wasn't going to say anything, but since Flora brought it up…

"Doesn't it bother you a little, knowing Ashlyn and Will used to be together?"

Flora looks nonplussed. "No, not at all. I know Will loves me and that his relationship with Ashlyn was just about convenience. They were always friends, and I'm glad they stayed friends. I also *adore* Ashlyn. You know that. So why would it bother me? Don't tell me *you're* jealous." Flora laughs incredulously.

I grunt, shrugging my shoulders and running my hand through my dark hair.

"I know all that, and I know I *shouldn't* be jealous, but I can't help it. They were together for almost a year, Flora. They were *with* each other. Don't get me wrong, you know how much I like Will, but still…" I trail off, feeling like an ass for even bringing this up. The more I talk about it, the crazier it sounds.

"Chase," Flora says, taking my hand from where it rests on the countertop. "You do know they were barely with each other when they were dating, right? They were both on location half a world apart most of that time. And also…" Flora blows out a breath, hesitant to continue, and I stand up straighter—knowing what she's about to say must be important. "I probably shouldn't be telling you this, as it really isn't my place, but…they *never* had sex."

I perk up at that. It's like a weight has been lifted off my shoulders.

I know I shouldn't care so much, but I do.

"They didn't?" I confirm as Flora squeezes my hand, and then drops it.

She shakes her head. "No, they didn't. Right after I found out that Ashlyn was Will's ex-girlfriend, I was jealous too. I'd been watching his movies, and when I got to the one he'd done with Ashlyn…" Flora pulls a face, wrinkling her nose. "It was *cringy,* and not because I had to watch them together, but because they had no chemistry. *At all.* When I mentioned it to Will he admitted they'd never done more than kiss."

I breathe out a sigh of relief. I'm still not thrilled that they kissed, but that's much, *much* better than thinking they'd had sex.

"Oh, that's…good," I mutter, still ashamed of my jealous behavior.

Flora nods. "I admit it might have been a little harder for me to accept if their relationship had been something more, but ultimately, it's not important. Will loves me and I love him. We all have pasts, Chase. It's the present, and the *future* that matters."

"You're right," I admit. "And I shouldn't care, anyway. It's not like we're together."

"But you want to be, don't you?"

There's no point in denying it, so I nod. "But Ashlyn would never…"

"Chase," Flora asserts, holding my eyes with a stern look. "Do you not see the way she looks at you? I know Ashlyn likes Hideaway Mountain and is happy to see Will and me and the baby, but she didn't come here for any of that. She came here for *you*."

Right as Flora finishes her statement, we hear Will and Ashlyn chatting from the other room as they approach the kitchen.

"Didn't get much outside to the table, did you?" Will teases Flora with a knowing look, eyes darting between me and her.

"Sorry, we were just catching up," Flora says, giving me a sly smile.

Could she be right?

Is it possible Ashlyn came here for *me*? That she wants me the same way I want her?

I glance over to Ashlyn as we all start to gather the food, drinks, and dishes to take outside.

She smiles at me like I hung the moon, that hungry look clear in her big hazel eyes.

How have I not seen it before? All this time I never even considered that my feelings could be reciprocated.

But now, it hits me like a rock to the head.

Ashlyn wants me. And I want her.

So, what the hell is stopping us?

ASHLYN

I can't recall the last time I felt happy like this.

Dinner with Chase, Will, Flora, and little Liam before he fell asleep was absolutely *perfect*. We chatted and laughed like the oldest of friends, giving me a sense of belonging I'm not sure I've ever felt before. Here, with these people, feels like home.

Like I'm exactly where I'm supposed to be.

It's a heady feeling that I've never experienced, not even before my dad died.

My father had cared for me in his way, but he'd been curt and exacting and not exactly loving. My mother died in a car crash when I was still a baby, and I think perhaps that's why he always kept me at arm's length.

Sometimes he'd remark how much I look like her with misery in his eyes, like my very existence was a painful reminder of the loss he'd never been able to cope with.

Growing up, my dad had lived for his work, and I spent most of my time either with nannies or on set with him when I was older, after begging him to take me along. I think he hoped I'd follow in his footsteps directing, but I'd fallen in love with acting instead.

I'll never forget the pained look in his eyes when I told him my dreams, even though he tried to hide his disappointment and promised to support me. My father always drew the line at giving me a part I didn't earn, however.

We agreed on that—I didn't want to be just another Hollywood nepo baby. I wanted to earn my way, so when he said he wouldn't intervene to get me roles or ever allow me to appear in one of his films I wholeheartedly agreed.

I was prepared to put the work in myself, and I did; even if some of the work I was forced to do made my father more ashamed of me than ever.

So no, I've never felt at home the way I do with this newfound family. I'm so glad I decided to step away from the limelight and come here.

Dinner wasn't only great conversation but also great food from the Hideaway Inn: freshly caught whitefish with herb-roasted potatoes and a seasonal salad, all locally sourced. Flora is passionate about her conservation work, and it shows in the delicious food from the pub she owns.

Desert had also been local. Palisade peaches, a yearly deliciously from the western slope of Colorado, were served with vanilla bean ice cream covered in whipped cream.

I'll admit I made eating it in front of Chase a bit of a show.

He sat next to me during dinner, tension simmering around us like I'd never experienced before. Our dynamic had changed—the transformation palpable.

Earlier, when I came back from my tour with Will, it felt like something between us had shifted. I saw it as soon as I walked back into the kitchen to join him and Flora.

Chase's usual stoic face had been filled with an emotion I couldn't quite place. The air between us buzzed with a current I could feel through every inch of my body, centering in my core, making my clit pulse with pent-up need.

Then when Will served us dessert, I seized the opportunity to test my recently acquired theory—that the new hungry look in Chase's eyes was want.

For *me*.

I started innocently enough, just running my spoon gingerly through the peaches and cream, looking up at Chase through my lashes until he met my eyes. Then I slowly brought the bite to my mouth, easing it through my lips while sighing at how good it was, taking extra time to *thoroughly* lick my spoon clean.

Chase had shifted in his seat, eyes darting from mine quickly when I went in for another bite, and I swear he cursed under his breath.

When Chase's eyes found mine again, it was as though he wanted to tease me right back. He picked up a slice of peach and dipped it into the ice cream before sliding it between his teeth, his tongue slowly coaxing it into his mouth and sucking at it until he finally swallowed. Then Chase licked his lips and remarked how tasty it was.

The earlier pulse I'd felt in my clit had become a needy ache.

I'm not sure if Flora and Will noticed what was happening between Chase and me, but I was relieved and excited when they excused themselves a moment later to check on Liam

As soon as they left the table, I mimicked what Chase had done, picking up a sweet piece of peach covered in cream, and sucking it down from between my fingers—making a performance of licking up the juice on my hand and lips after.

Chase didn't even try to hold back his groan at my seductive move and pushed his chair closer to me. He angled himself to look directly into my eyes, his filled with lust, pupils dilated with need.

"You missed a little," he said, voice gruff. "Right here." Chase then lifted his hand to wipe off a bit of cream from my lip, that I may or may not have deliberately left there.

As his pointer finger met my lip, I grabbed his thick wrist. When Chase started to pull back, the dollop of cream on his fingertip, I held him to me—opening my lips and licking it off him. My tongue had darted out and swirled while I sucked gently, hallowing my cheeks just enough to make the reference clear.

"Ashlyn…*fuck*," he growled, and I gave him a saucy smile in return. Chase had leaned in at that, and I was sure he was going to kiss me. But then our hosts walked back out, and the moment was lost.

Not long after, Will and Flora admitted to being exhausted and ready to call it a night. They walked us to the door and said goodbye, a knowing look in both their eyes, especially Flora's.

Now, Chase and I are together in his truck driving back to my rental. Since what happened at dinner things have become a bit…*awkward* between us, but the heat is still there. I can practically feel it emanating from Chase as he drives.

His pine-and-cedar scent is *everywhere* in his truck, fueling my arousal further and making me squirm uncomfortably in my seat. My eyes keep drifting down to Chase's crotch, and I swear the bulge in his pants is bigger than it was earlier (yes, I will admit I've been shameless in my perusal of his body).

Obviously, I'm not the only one incredibly turned on.

I keep having to rub my thighs together, trying to get some friction to my aching center, and I'm so wet I can feel my panties sticking to my sex.

We've not said a word to each other when Chase opens

the remote gate and pulls onto the drive leading to my rental. Part of me had hoped Chase would invite me to stay with him, and I'd even considered asking but didn't have the nerve. Now knowing I'll have to spend the entire night away from him, pent up and practically trembling with want, makes me want to cry in frustration.

Chase turns to me and smiles as he shifts his truck into park, and I do my best to smile in return without revealing how much I'm burning for him.

"Where is Beau staying tonight?" he asks, referring to my bodyguard who's leaving in the morning.

"There's a pool house out back, he's staying there for the night," I answer, noting how some of the tension in Chase's shoulders eases at my words. I know Chase likes Beau and is fully aware our relationship is strictly professional, but I get the feeling he still doesn't like the idea of another man sleeping too close to me.

Chase nods as he unbuckles his seat belt and climbs out of the truck, coming to my side and helping me down.

We walk silently towards the house, neither of us sure how to move through this tension between us. I unlock and swing the door open, turning to Chase before entering.

"So," I say, hesitant at first and then finally craning my head up to look Chase in the eyes.

I'm fairly tall for a woman at 5'8", but Chase is practically a giant and still over a foot taller.

I love how small and delicate he makes me feel. Though I've always been naturally slender, I have a curvy waist, butt, and hips that I work hard to keep toned, especially after I was accused of being *"too fat,"* for a couple of roles in my early years.

I've learned to love my body, but I'm also used to being bigger than many of the men I work with. So, I adore how tiny and almost *fragile* I feel with Chase.

I love knowing that he could protect me from almost anything.

When Chase meets my eyes, I'm momentarily struck dumb, but eventually force out words despite my desire-ravaged brain.

"Tomorrow I was thinking it might be nice to go for a hike together. If that sound good to you?"

Chase nods again, smiling wide enough that lines appear near his eyes. He looks so happy in this moment, happier than I've ever seen him.

I do my best to capture the look on his face in a mental picture I can keep always.

"If a hike is what my princess wants, then a hike is what she'll get."

I take a sharp breath at his words. Sure, Chase calls me princess all the time, but he's never referred to me as *his princess*.

Not even once.

I'd have remembered that.

"Really?" I sigh, blinking up at him in an attempt to clear the giddiness from my eyes. "I'm *your* princess?"

Chase shrugs like it's no big deal. "Yeah. If you want to be."

I nod furiously and grab Chase by his shirt, pulling him down to me until I can easily reach his shoulders. I slide my hands up and wind my arms around his neck, crushing my lips to his in a wet, hungry kiss.

Chase groans and takes control of the kiss almost immediately, his arms wrapping around my waist and pulling me against his hard chest. I can feel every ridge of his muscle beneath my taunt nipples, his solid length pressing against my stomach, and it's enough to make me moan into his mouth. Chase takes advantage of my parted lips and thrusts his tongue in to meet mine, gliding across in a silky slide and angling himself to go deeper.

Chase is as ravenous for me as I am for him.

I wrap my lips around his hot tongue and suck him further inside, demonstrating just how much I'd love to feel another part of him deep within me.

Chase pulls away at that, cursing under his breath, his hand coming to my cheek and caressing it—a gentle contrast to his rough, demanding kiss.

"Ashlyn…*damn*…" Chase trails off as our eyes again meet.

The look he gives me is completely open, and for the first time, I feel like I can see *everything;* almost down to his soul. I know it's a vulnerability he doesn't show many other people.

Suddenly, the way Chase has been pining for me seems crystal clear. I feel almost foolish for not noticing it before.

I can tell Chase is ready to let me in, ready to make me his in every way.

His princess.

The only question is, am I ready to let him?

* * *

Something was burning.

I'd been tossing and turning in bed for the past hour, thinking about that kiss and why the hell I'd let Chase leave. So, at first, I thought I must be dreaming.

Chase had been confused when I'd pulled away following our kiss, telling him a quick goodnight and that I'd see him in the morning. I still don't understand my actions, but I suppose a part of me had panicked since it felt so unexpected.

Arriving in town and almost immediately realizing the man who's become my best friend lusts for me as much as I lust for him *hadn't* been anywhere on my bingo card. I've wanted Chase for so long I didn't know what to do once I had him.

I've never had a real relationship with someone I truly *wanted* to be with. Every so-called boyfriend in my past was just a career ploy or a means to get the Hollywood gossip factory to leave me alone. My prior experiences with intimacy have been either unwanted, uncomfortable, or performed on a movie set.

I have *no idea* how to do this, and I can only hope pulling away from Chase tonight didn't ruin things before they could even start.

When I'd finally drifted off it had been to images of Chase in his firefighter uniform, his salt-and-pepper hair rucked, shirt sooty and torn, revealing glimpses of the tattoos I've seen peeking below his shirtsleeves.

Chase had left me so hot and achy from his kiss that I'd eventually succumbed to getting myself off. My fingers had worked my wet clit until I'd found release and fallen into a fitful slumber.

So, when I initially noticed it, I thought the smoky smell must have been conjured by my lust-muddled brain. Perhaps I'd been dreaming of Chase saving me from a blaze?

But no, I realize quickly as I open my heavy eyes, bringing my sluggish brain back online. I wasn't dreaming.

The fire alarm is blaring, and smoke is indeed filling my bedroom—its acrid odor making me cough and sputter as I fumble for the phone on my bedside table, smoke stinging my eyes as I search for it blindly in the dark.

My fingers finally wrap around it, and I pull myself out of bed, throwing the covers to the floor as I stumble forward, searching for escape.

The only light emanates through the windows of the room—a red-orange glow from outside. I approach slowly to get a better look and find flames licking up one entire side of the house. It's hard to see through the smoke streaming in, and the heat is intense, but I manage to make out Beau as he flies out of the pool house below. I see him yelling as he rushes around beneath me. I can't hear him, but I'm guessing he's calling for me.

Hand still gripped tightly on my phone, eyes burning with tears, I manage to turn toward the closed bedroom door. I practically fall against it, and finding it cool to the touch I fling it open and rush out into the hall, smoke following behind me. I'm able to breathe easier now though, finding the corridor and stairs free of fire, the only smoke billowing out from the place I was sleeping.

I fly down the stairs and towards the front door, a part of my sleep and adrenaline-addled mind still trying to grasp this reality.

Am I sure this isn't a dream?

I accidentally bite down on my tongue as I run, the metallic taste of blood filling my mouth.

No, this *definitely* isn't a dream.

This hellish nightmare is very real.

CHASE

I'm fisting my cock when my phone vibrates loudly on the bedside table.

I'm not proud of it, I tried to resist as long as I could, but even after a whiskey and a cold shower, my blood was still too hot for sleep. I knew the only way I was going to get any shut-eye was if I jacked off to images of what I *wished* had happened after Ashlyn kissed me.

She'd tasted better than I imagined possible, just like the peaches and cream she teased me with at dinner. I almost blew my load in my jeans when she sucked my finger at the table, the only thing preventing me from spreading her out and feasting between her legs then and there was the fact we were at our friend's home.

The air between us had been thick with sexual tension throughout the meal, and for the first time, I was able to fully see what Flora had pointed out.

Ashlyn's desire for me seemed clear as day in her pretty hazel eyes, leaving me wondering how the hell I'd been so blind to it before.

Had that look always been there?

Was I *really* just now seeing it?

I didn't want to waste any more time now that Ashlyn was here with me, so I intended to tell her my feelings once we left Flora and Will's. But then after our little game with desert at the table, I seemed to lose all capabilities of speech on the drive—the air vibrating with unspoken desire the entire way down the mountain.

Finally, I found my words and felt emboldened to call Ashlyn *my* princess for the first time out loud, and I guess that was all she needed to hear.

She was fierce and hungry when she grabbed me, pulling my willing lips down to hers. Ashlyn had felt so soft and perfect in my arms—it had taken everything in me not to rip off her dress, throw her over my shoulder, and carry her off to bed.

I'd held myself in check mostly because Ashlyn had initiated the kiss, and I thought surely after the passion we shared she'd ask me to stay.

So, I was more than a little surprised when she didn't.

I pulled away for a second to take a breath, muttering something to her I don't even recall, and that brief pause had been enough to dim the fire in her eyes.

Ashlyn had pulled back and looked at her feet, breathing heavily as she seemed to gather her thoughts. After a moment she met my eyes, quickly saying goodnight and that she'd be ready early the next day for our hike.

She then went inside and shut the door, leaving me confused and *wanting*. I spent the entire drive back to my place fighting the urge to turn around, march into her bedroom, and pick up where we'd left off.

Instead, I applied pressure to my dick with one hand in an attempt to dampen my frustration and drove with the other, damn near running off the road more times than once before finally arriving at my cabin.

Once home I considered texting her, but decided it might be best to let sleeping dogs lie.

Something had spooked her, and though I wasn't sure what exactly it had been, I didn't want to push her away further. I'd be seeing her early tomorrow anyway, and we'd have plenty of time to talk about things then.

My resolve to leave her alone for the evening, unfortunately, didn't transfer to my cock. So, after lying in bed with blue balls for what seemed like an eternity, I'd taken myself in hand. One squeeze of my shaft had precum bubbling out from the tip, and I used it as lubrication while stroking roughly up and down, thinking about what I'd say to Ashlyn in the morning—confessing how much I wanted her and all the filthy things I longed to do to her beautiful body.

A quick release had seemed inevitable, but then I heard my phone. I guess all I needed to calm my raging hard-on was to roll over and see Javier Sanchez's name flashing across the screen.

I drop my softening dick and fumble to answer. Since I'm on vacation and Javier is the acting chief, I know something must be extremely wrong for him to be calling at nearly one in the morning.

"What's wrong?" I ask as I pick up my phone, not bothering with a greeting. My voice is horse and gravelly, sounding half asleep, even as adrenaline starts shooting through my body. I know in my bones whatever he has to say, it can't be good.

I hear a sharp intake of breath on the other line before Javier speaks.

"Let me start by saying Ashlyn is okay. There was a fire at the place she's staying, but she's fine. She's right here next to me."

God bless Javier for not beating around the bush, and though I'm relieved to hear Ashlyn is okay, that doesn't stop the blood from freezing in my veins at the thought that she almost wasn't—that something terrible had almost happened to her.

"A fire?" I exclaim, already launching myself out of bed, putting my phone on speaker as I flip on the lights and quickly dress.

"Yeah. We got a call from the alarm company and were already en route when Ashlyn's bodyguard called 911. He'd woken up to the smell of smoke, and luckily so had Ashlyn. She got out of the house before the fire spread too far. It looks like maybe an electrical issue, but of course, we won't be sure until there's an investigation."

I nod, and then remembering Javier can't see me I grunt out a response. "I'm on my way," I say, rushing out my bedroom door clad in sweats and a black T-shirt, shoving my feet in shoes and grabbing my keys as I head to my truck. "You said Ashlyn is with you, can I talk to her?"

I hear a rustling and then the sweetest sound to ever fill my ears. "Chase?" Ashlyn's voice is weak. She's shaken up.

"Princess," I reply as I start my truck, phone connecting to the radio Bluetooth. "I'm on my way. Are you okay? Did a medic check you out?"

"I'm okay," she practically whispers, "Javier checked me himself, said you'd kill him if he let anyone else, and I'm alright. I inhaled a bit of smoke but my oxygen levels were fine."

A weak smile crosses my face at her words, glad that Javier took care of her. He knows me too well—I'd have been livid if he'd let some young rookie put his hands on my girl.

"That's good," I say, turning off my rocky driveway and rushing up the road. "And Beau? He's alright too?"

"Yes," Ashlyn says. "He mostly just seems pissed that he didn't get to me sooner, but we were both asleep when the fire started."

I smile a little again. Beau's a good man, and I've no doubt he's full of guilt. *I* certainly am. I never should have left Ashlyn alone tonight.

"Chase…" Ashlyn starts, her voice cracking. "I'm okay, really, I am. But I was so *scared*. I thought I might die…die without ever telling you…" Her voice breaks at that, a sob escaping as Ashlyn begins to cry.

"Shh, princess," I soothe, wishing I was there to hold her. "I'll be there soon, and then you're coming home with me."

With me, where she should have been from the start—wrapped safely in my arms.

If I have my way, Ashlyn will never sleep away from me again.

* * *

I ARRIVE a few minutes later after speeding up the mountain and am greeted by a site that would have stopped my heart if I didn't already know that Ashlyn's okay.

The place she's staying is surrounded by fire trucks, and one entire side of the house is burnt and smoking—the side where her room was. I park quickly and rush out, passing an ambulance and waving briefly at a couple of medics I know.

I need to find Ashlyn and see for myself she's alright.

When I round the ambulance my eyes first land on Javier, dressed in full gear, and then dart to the smaller figure next to him.

Ashlyn is huddled with her head down, hand clinging tightly to a blanket wrapped around her shoulders. She looks up as I approach, and the relieved smile I see on her face makes my heart race. I close the distance between us in a few strides, and she opens her arms, wrapping me in the blanket with her as she clings to my waist.

"Ashlyn, thank god," I sigh, tucking my chin and kissing

the top of her head. Her auburn hair is loose around her shoulders, and she smells like smoke. It makes my entire body clench, reminding me how close I came to losing her.

"Chase, I'm so glad you're here," she sighs, her small hands clutching at my shirt as the blanket begins to slide off her shoulders. I let go of her briefly to grab and wrap it back around her, and then pull her into my chest.

Even though it's technically still summer, the nights are already getting colder, and Ashlyn is covered only in a skimpy pair of sleep shorts and a tank top. I don't want her to get cold, and I also don't want any of the other men here ogling her.

Speaking of...

"Javier, everyone here knows to keep their mouths shut about Ashlyn, right? The last thing we need after this is a bunch of people in town knowing she's here and then having the paparazzi descend on her."

Javier nods. "Yeah, I told them to stay quiet if they want to keep their jobs. Don't worry, everyone here has too much respect for you to do something that would put your girl in danger." I nod, the stubble on my chin rubbing against the top of Ashlyn's head, catching briefly in her hair.

"Good," I reply. Before today, I'd have denied that Ashlyn is *my* girl, but after everything that's happened, I want *everyone* to know she's mine; if they do anything to threaten her safety, they'll be answering to me. "Is Beau still here? I'd like to ask him about what he saw."

Ashlyn shakes her head and looks up at me, resting her chin on my chest.

"Javier already talked to him, and a cop got a statement, but he left a couple of minutes ago. We all told him it's not his fault, but I think he's feeling pretty guilty, and maybe didn't want to face you. He kept saying how he let us both down."

Another confirmation of what a good man Beau is, and I certainly have no ill will for him. I know none of this was his fault.

"It sounds to me like he did everything he could. Where did he go? It's a little late to try and get a flight."

"I called Ella, and she was able to get him a room at the inn. She went there for the night," Javier answers.

I nod. Ella manages the lodge at the Hideaway Inn and is close with Javier. Her dad used to be the fire chief before me, and both Javier and I were close to the man. I think that's why he's never made a move on Ella, even though everyone in Hideaway Valley knows the two are clearly in love.

"We should get you out of here," I say to Ashlyn, squeezing her more tightly to me as we speak. "Are you ready?" Ashlyn nods into my chest, and I swiftly grab her under her long legs and hoist her into my arms, preparing to carry her to my truck.

"Chase!" she cries, and it's a relief to hear some of the spirit back in her voice. "I can walk, you know."

"You're not wearing any shoes," I growl, hugging her more tightly to my chest. "I've got you."

Ashlyn sighs and burrows her cheek against me as I begin to turn, speaking to Javier before I walk away.

"You'll let us know when the investigation is concluded, and we can come back for her things?"

Javier nods. "Of course. Although, I'm afraid there might not be much left. The room Ashlyn was in seems to have sustained some of the worst of the damage." I growl again, wanting to hit someone or something for almost hurting my princess.

But if it *was* an electrical issue, there isn't anyone I can take it out on. Except maybe whoever installed the faulty wiring. Or better yet, that *fucking property manager*. It's his whole job to make sure the places he rents are safe for guests.

Maybe I should have a word with him...

I'm pulled out of my spiraling thoughts when Ashlyn speaks.

"It's okay. I can always get new stuff, and at least I managed to save my phone," she pats the pocket of her pajama shorts.

That's my girl, always looking at the positive, even during what is probably one of the scariest moments of her life.

God, I love this woman.

We say goodbye to Javier and I carry Ashlyn to my truck, making sure she is safely buckled in before I return to the driver's seat and pull out onto the dark road.

At first, we're silent—Ashlyn staring out the window and into the night. I wonder what she's thinking, and if maybe she wants to go home to California. I couldn't blame her for wanting to leave after all this, so I ask.

"No," she replies, sounding surprised. "Do you want me to leave?"

I shake my head vehemently. "Of course, I don't," I answer. "If it were up to me, I'd keep you here forever. I just wasn't sure if you'd want to leave after what happened."

"I'm not going to let a little fire ruin my vacation," Ashlyn tries to lighten the mood, cracking a small smile as she turns from the window to look at me. "I'm sure I can find somewhere else to stay…"

"No," I interrupt. "You're staying with me, princess. I should have asked you to stay with me from the beginning, I just wasn't sure you'd want to."

Ashlyn brightens further at my words. "Really? That's what I wanted too. I was going to ask you, but I didn't want to impose."

I laugh. "We've both been idiots about all this, haven't we? Pining away for each other, too afraid to say what we want." Ashlyn nods at my words. "Well, let me make myself crystal clear now, princess. I *want you* to stay at my cabin with me, and not just in my cabin, but in *my bed*. We don't have to do anything if you're not ready, but I want you next to me so I know you're safe. I want you as close to me as possible for the rest of the time you're here. To put it simply, I just *want you*, Ashlyn."

"I want you too, Chase," Ashlyn says as I pull into the driveway of my house. I waste no time getting out, swinging her back into my arms, and carrying her inside. I have to shift her weight in my arms slightly when I open the door, but she's so light against me it doesn't take much effort.

Once the door is closed behind us I set Ashlyn down, this time dragging it out. I let her feel *every* part of my hardness against her softness along the way.

"We'll get you some new clothes or whatever you need tomorrow," I say as I look into her gorgeous eyes, framed by long dark lashes. I run my thumb across her plump pink lips and up to her cheek, tucking her hair behind her ear. "But for now, I bet you'd like to get cleaned up, get the smell of smoke off you. How does a bath sound?"

"A bath sounds divine," she replies, catching my big wrist as I go to pull away, keeping my hand on her cheek.

I nod, even though part of me disagrees.

A bath might be nice, but it isn't divine.

Divine is having Ashlyn here with me. *Divine* is her touch on my bare skin.

Divine is how I intend to make Ashlyn feel when she's ready to let me inside her.

ASHLYN

Chase's home is a lot like the man himself—attractive, large, and a bit imposing from the outside; warm, inviting, and beautiful on the inside.

It's built of logs which are visible throughout, and opens to a vaulted entryway and staircase. I've seen glimpses of it from our video calls, and though I'm excited to get the grand tour and see the entire place firsthand, right now all I want is to clean up and soothe my frayed nerves. And the bath Chase has offered sounds perfect.

I follow Chase up the stairs, disappointed to no longer be in his arms, ridiculous though it may be to expect the man to carry me everywhere. When he'd put me down a few moments ago, I'd felt every inch of him against my scantily clad body, and for a brief second, it made me forget all about the fire I just narrowly escaped.

I think poor Beau may have been even more shaken up than I am, however, even though he wasn't as close to the fire. He would barely meet my eyes when the emergency crew arrived, his guilt at not being able to prevent what happened evident.

As Chase said though, there is no reason for him to feel that way. We were asleep when it happened, and both he and Chase had thoroughly checked the house to ensure I'd be safe. They both may be experts in their chosen professions, but if what Javier said is true, and the fire was caused by a faulty electoral system, there's no way they would have noticed the problem.

I was relieved when Javier arrived on the scene tonight with his crew—maybe not as relieved as I'd have felt if he'd been Chase, but I met Javier on my first visit to Hideaway, and knowing he and Chase are close friends made me certain I'd be safe in his hands.

I want to believe what Javier said is true; that the fire was just an accident of bad wiring. But I can't seem to shake the feeling that it was more sinister than that.

Could my stalker, *"Eternally Yours,"* have found out where I am? Could he have been the one to start the fire?

In a few of his letters, he referenced things like his "smoldering desire" and how he wanted me to "burn with him in the blaze of his love." So, the fire theme certainly fits.

But how could he possibly know where I am? No one other than Beau and the pilots who flew me here have any clue I left L.A. Not even my agent and other so-called Hollywood friends know I'm gone yet.

I brush the suspicions of my stalker off as Chase leads me into his large primary suite. I'm in enough shock as it is from my ordeal. If I start to focus on the remote possibility that I was followed here, I'll just make myself crazy.

We pass Chase's gigantic bed, and enter into the adjoining, equally huge on-suite. It makes sense that for a man of his proportions, everything would have to come in extra, *extra-* large sizes.

Including, I bet, one *specific* part of his anatomy.

A part I felt pushed up against me earlier.

"I have a few different bath bombs," Chase says, pulling me from my increasingly dirty thoughts as he grabs a box from beneath the sink. "Lavender vanilla, peppermint, jasmine, cherry blossom..."

I giggle as he paws through the different options.

"*You* have bath bombs?" I ask. "I didn't know you liked baths so much. I'm trying to picture you soaking in cherry blossom-scented bubbles."

Chase smirks. "I do enjoy the occasional bath. It's good for achy muscles. I *am* an old man, after all." I scoff at his *"old man"* comment. "I even made sure to get this extra-large tub installed so my feet wouldn't hang off the edge," he gestures to the huge soaking tub on the other side of the sink. It's so big it looks like it would fit at least three people.

Or, one very large person and one smaller person...

"I will also have you know," Chase continues, again pulling me from my lusty thoughts, "that cherry blossom happens to be my favorite scent. It reminds me of *you*."

I gasp a little at that. I've never told Chase that cherry blossom is my favorite perfume, and he wouldn't have smelled it on me again until today.

So that means he must have remembered it from the only day we ever spent together in person before now.

"You remembered what I smell like?" I ask, smiling up at him.

Chase nods. "Everything about you was vividly imprinted on me the day we met, Ashlyn. You were unlike anyone I'd ever known before. You made me feel...you *still* make me feel, things I never even imagined possible."

I squeeze his hand as my smile grows, suddenly unsure how to respond to this sweet declaration.

"Well," I say, my voice dipping low and quiet, "then I guess I'll take cherry blossom for my bath."

Chase nods again and brings my hand to his lips, placing

a quick kiss on my palm before moving to the tub and turning on the faucets.

The hot water begins to immediately steam up the room as we wait for the bath to fill.

"I'll go get you something to wear," Chase says. "Is a T-shirt okay? I doubt anything else I have will fit."

"That's perfect," I answer as he leaves the room.

Noticing the water level is high enough now for me to start soaking, I start to strip off my clothes and get in. I'm not wearing anything other than my sleep shorts and tank, so within a few seconds, I'm naked and stepping into the tub, right as Chase reenters the room.

"I hope this…" he starts, but quickly loses his words when he sees me halfway in the tub and lowering myself down into the warm water.

He clears his throat. "I'll just leave you to it then."

"Wait," I say, and he freezes, the desire clear in the depths of his oceanic eyes. "I forgot the bath bomb."

Chase picks it up from the counter, unwraps it, and brings it to me, eyes darting to and then away from my exposed body.

Always the gentleman, Chase.

Even when I don't want him to be.

He drops the pink-colored cylinder into the water; it bubbles and fizzes and fills the air with the sweet smell of cherries. Chase turns to leave again, but I grab him by the wrist to halt his progress.

"*Stay,*" I practically whisper. "Stay with me."

"Princess," he moans, "I'm not sure if you're ready for what my staying would mean. You've been through so much tonight already…"

"I'm fine," I cut him off. "And I know what I want. I want *you*. Life's too short to waste even a moment."

Chase sighs. "You know how much I want you too, but…

what about earlier, before the fire? You kissed me and then you couldn't get away fast enough. Something made you hesitate, and I don't…"

"Chase," I say, tugging him closer until he sits on the edge of the tub. "I didn't hesitate because I wasn't sure if I wanted you. *I do.* I always have, from the first day we met."

Chase's face, which had fallen into a frown cracks at that. He smiles.

"Really? You didn't think I was an argonaut jackass for making you stay so close to me when we went to find Flora? Or when I demanded to come back with you to make sure you were okay after?"

I shake my head, recalling that day a year ago when I first met both Chase and Flora.

I'd come to the Hideaway Inn to check on and apologize to Will, and he left with me briefly so I could explain away from prying eyes and the risk of being recognized. Flora didn't know why Will had gone with me, and so mistakenly thought he had left her. In her anger and sadness, Flora has taken off up the mountain to hike in a rain storm that was threatening to cause a flood.

When Will and I arrived back at the inn, we'd been greeted by Chase, Javier, and Ella, who told us Flora had left and they were getting ready to go after her. But Will and I insisted on going instead; he needed to get her back, and since the entire misunderstanding was my fault to begin with, I thought it was my responsibility to help fix it.

Chase had then also demanded to come, and at the time I believed it was just because he was a firefighter and thought it was his responsibility to ensure my safety.

Looking back on it now, it seems obvious he felt something for me other than duty right from the start. Chase captivated me immediately too. It was a feeling I'd never experienced before.

When I left him and Hideaway Mountain the next day to return to California, a part of my heart stayed with him—a part I knew I would never get back.

"Okay," I finally answer, "maybe I did think you were a little bit stubborn, bossy, and extremely protective considering I was a stranger, but I also thought that was just because you were so good at your job. I mostly thought you were the most handsome man I'd ever met. There was something in your eyes too, something I'd never encountered before, and something I knew I would never encounter again. I've always wanted you, Chase."

"I've always wanted you too, Ashlyn," Chase replies, stroking my hand where it still rests on his, moving up gradually to massage my upper arm and then shoulder. "I moment I saw you, I was done for. You're the only one for me."

"Good," I say, reaching for his other arm while he continues to massage me, trying to pull him closer. I get him halfway to my lips before he stops, hesitating again.

"Why then," he asks, furrowing his brow in concern, "if you've always wanted me, why did you pull away from me before?"

"Because I…I guess I panicked a little. I've not been truly open and intimate like this with anyone, *ever*. The sexual experiences I've had were either awful, awkward, or purely acting for the screen."

"What exactly are you saying?" Chase asks. "You're not a…"

"Virgin? No," I finish for him. "But it's been almost a decade since my only time having *real* sex, so I might as well be."

Chase's eyes are boring into mine and I can tell he isn't going to let this go without further discussion.

As much as I don't want to talk about my past with sex,

and as awful as exhuming those buried memories and feelings will be, I know it's something he needs to hear.

If I want Chase to fully understand me, and if I want us to have a real relationship and a real future, I have to tell him everything about me. I need to be brave—to pull it all out into the light where we *both* can see.

Even the most painful, deeply hidden parts.

"I've told you a little bit about my father and my family already. He was a director, and the Addison's have been in Hollywood since practically the dawn of film. When I decided to become an actress, my father and I agreed that he wouldn't help me in any way beyond assisting with some initial payments for an agent. My name gave me enough recognition to get my foot in the door, but after that, I couldn't get any lead, or even any *decent* roles. When I was 19, I'd been working hard for two years, but hadn't managed to snag anything beyond a few supporting parts, and was desperate for something more, something *better*. When another actress I was acquainted with landed a *huge* role, even though she was brand new and hadn't done anything close to it before, I wanted to know how she'd snagged it. So, I asked. She was also young, but extremely…*forthright*, and unabashedly shared she'd slept with the director to get the part. I wasn't so naïve that I didn't know that sort of thing happens in Hollywood, but I was still shocked. This particular director was well-known and very successful, with several Oscars to his name. He was also almost three times her age. She could tell I was taken aback and slightly disgusted by her disclosure, but she wasn't the type to take it personally. Instead, she told me that the same director had a son who was following in his father's footsteps, and currently casting for a film he was co-directing. When she told me more about the movie, and I realized how huge getting a part in it would be for my career, I was desperate to get an audition. She said she'd put a word in for me, and thought maybe if I got *close* with the younger director, the son, I might increase my chances of getting a role. So, that's what I did."

I pause for a moment and look at Chase to see his reaction. His jaw is tight and there's anger in his eyes.

He already sees where this story is going.

I take a deep breath and continue, spitting out the rest of my shameful tale as quickly as I can manage.

"I went to the audition she arranged for me, and then I went out with the director's son on a date. He told me if I agreed to be his girlfriend, he would give me the lead in the movie. He was trying to make a name for himself in the industry and knew being attached to a young actress from a well-known Hollywood family would be good for his reputation. When we slept together, I cried almost the entire time. So, he never tried to have sex with me again. He did like to have me give him blowjobs though, and when we eventually broke up, he started to spread rumors about how good I was at it. I dated a few other guys who promised me parts in exchange for *that*, but eventually, I made enough of a name for myself that I didn't have to do those types of things anymore to get the roles I wanted. My other few boyfriends, including Will, were relationships in name only. Being linked publicly benefited our careers and helped to keep negative rumors out of the tabloids."

When I finish, I realize the tub is almost overflowing, so I lean forward and turn off the water.

When I lean back, I see that Chase's entire body is clenched, and he looks like he's ready to march right out of here, find every man that ever hurt me, and make them pay. I adore that he's so protective of me—like a huge, handsome avenging angel—but this is all in my past, and that's where I want to keep it. There's nothing Chase or anyone else can do to change it now.

"Who were these men?" Chase forces out between his teeth, jaw tight. "They should pay for what they did to you. I should fucking *kill them* for touching you."

"It doesn't matter now," I answer, and Chase furiously shakes his head in disagreement. "It was a long time ago. Besides, I agreed to everything that I did with them. Inside, I might not have wanted to. Inside, I might've been screaming for it to stop, but I never said anything out loud. I went along with it, just so I could get those stupid parts. You must think I'm such a fool. You must be disgusted."

"Are you kidding me?" Chase exclaims, sounding offended. "You were young and desperate, not a fool, and the only thing I find disgusting is the way those men took advantage of you. Even if you went along with it, what they did to you wasn't right. You must know that."

I nod weakly. "I guess I do, but I would still rather forget about it, and just leave it in the past where it belongs. Okay?" I capture Chase's eyes with my own, my hand clasping his. I take a breath and wait a moment until he relaxes slightly, and nods begrudgingly before going on. "Now you know why I hesitated earlier, and that it had nothing to do with my feelings for you. I *want* to be with you, Chase. *Right now,*" I tug him down toward me again and he finally gives in, meeting my lips in a gentle kiss.

"You know," he says, lips brushing mine as he speaks, "it's been a long time for me too. Five years. And no other woman has ever made me *half* as hard as you do. I might embarrass myself and explode as soon as I touch you."

"Don't care," I say between hot little kisses to his lips, chin, and cheeks. "If you do, we'll just try again and *again* and *again* until we get it right. Now strip and get in here already."

Chase grins and pulls away, standing to his full remarkable height.

He starts by stripping off his shirt and revealing the tattoos I've only seen hints of before. There's a half sleeve on one muscular arm depicting the mountain valley and his firehouse number—other designs scattering across his arms and onto one side of his ribs.

His sweatpants go next, and he must have been in a hurry to get to me earlier, as he doesn't have anything on underneath them. Every part of Chase is molded to perfection; abs clenching as he moves, engraved v-lines a tantalizing map leading towards his *very* impressive cock.

Impressive might be an understatement.

Like everything else on the man, Chase's erection is *huge* —his thick length standing at attention and weeping from the flushed head.

I can't suppress the whimper that escapes me at the sight of it. I'm awed and also a little frightened.

I've never been a big fan of the other dicks I've seen in my life, but this one is *beautiful*. I long to have it inside me, but I'm also not quite sure how it will fit. The only other guy I've been with had a much smaller penis, and the entire experience was so bad and over so fast I'm not even sure he penetrated me completely.

But there is *no way* Chase's cock won't penetrate fully. He may very well rip me in half.

He must see the stunned look on my face as he smiles at me seductively, and gestures for me to scoot up in the tub. I shuffle forward to make space for him behind me, and Chase climbs in.

As he lowers himself into the water, I can feel every rigid part of him against my back, his muscular legs straddling my body. Chase lifts me slightly by the hips and onto his lap, his steel length notching in the space between my ass and pussy.

Chase keeps his big hands at my waist as he kisses from my shoulder to my neck, fingers massaging and digging into my sides as they drift up my body. He licks a stripe up to my ear and tugs the lobe gently with his teeth, his hot breath making me tremble in his arms.

"You feel so fucking good against me princess. So beautiful. So perfect. This is exactly where you belong," he whispers, voice gravely and laced with lust.

I nod. "Yes," I manage to sigh, all other words catching in my throat as his hand moves up to cup my achy breasts, molding and massaging them with his palms as his fingers play with my nipples.

I writhe against him, and rock my hips once, making his hard cock slide between my folds. It feels so good that I do it again, rolling back farther until his tip hits my swollen clit, pulsing and begging for attention.

It must feel good for Chase too, as he groans and thrusts himself forward as I rock back, his calloused hands tugging harder at my breasts while he sucks and bites a bruise at the base of my neck, the stubble on his cheek scraping against my sensitized skin.

"You're drenched for me," Chase says, thrusting up harder as one hand snakes from my chest down to my needy center. "Even in the water, I can feel how wet you are. Is all this cream for me?" His broad fingers have found my clit, and he's rubbing it in teasing circles, making more arousal pour from my tight hole.

"All for you," I reply, leaning my head back against his chest, shifting my hips slightly, and parting my legs further to give him better access to my sex. "No one's ever made me feel like this before."

Chase grunts and starts to increase the pressure on my clit with his thumb, his middle finger finding my entrance and probing at it gently before sinking inside. His fingers are long and wide and I cry out at the intrusion.

It's a blissful pain and I want more, so I pump my hips harder until Chase gets the hint, adding a second finger and plunging even deeper, rubbing at my inner walls until he finds the spongey bundle of nerves inside that makes me desperate to come.

My breaths are coming out in short pants, and I can feel the beating of Chase's heart behind me as he fucks me harder with his fingers, crooking one inside while the other flicks my clit.

I chase my orgasm up, up, *up*—tightness building in my core until finally, with one more pulse of his fingers, *I release*.

My body shudders and shakes, hands digging into the sides of Chase's thighs, nails scraping at his skin.

"Chase!" I cry as the blood rushes to my ears, light exploding behind my closed lids in an electric rush of pleasure.

"That's it, princess," he moans into my ear, breath hot as he nips at the lobe. "You come for me so prettily. You're so fucking perfect."

Chase continues to rub me through my climax until I become too sensitive and pull away with a small whimper. My body is spent and satisfied, but Chase is still hard and tense behind me.

He adjusts me on his lap until his cock is sliding fully against my seam, brushing my sensitive nub as he guides me back and forth. I rock my hips to meet his motion, bending my knees and placing my feet on the bottom of the tub as the water sloshes around us.

"Touch me, princess…please," he begs, voice ragged and desperate with need.

I wrap my fingers around his erection and rub my palm along his shaft as he continues to move up and down beneath me. It only takes a few strokes before he comes, releasing hot ropes between us into the water, cock throbbing in my hand until he's completely rung out.

I can't help but feel a slight sense of loss as I watch his spend float and disperse in the tub.

It's a primal, biological response.

I want that *inside* me. I don't want any of it going to waste.

Chase's seed belongs in my womb.

I'm pulled from my thoughts as Chase jerks out of my hand, the touch becoming too intense. He sighs and leans back against the tub, turning my body in his arms until we're face to face and I'm straddling him.

"That was a good place to start," he says, kissing me hard on the lips, claiming my mouth as his own. "But next time," he continues as he pulls away, "next time I come, I want it to be deep inside of you. That's where I belong princess. You're *mine*."

I nod and claim him right back, arms wrapping tightly around his neck, kissing him with a lifetime's worth of pent-up passion.

I couldn't agree more. I belong to Chase.

Chase belongs to me.

And no matter what happens after this moment, I *know* that's how it will *always* be.

CHASE

I wake up to a hot little mouth on me.

A warm tongue licks up my shaft and swirls around the head of my cock as I slowly drift back to consciousness—hazy memories from last night drifting through my sleep-drugged mind.

As much as I wanted to fuck Ashlyn senseless in the bathtub, her story about her past sexual experiences gave me pause. I also knew that despite her protests she was exhausted and had been through enough. The last thing she needed was my massive cock splitting her in two. I'm a big man, and I'm well aware that I can be a lot to handle.

I want the first time we're together to be *perfect*, not just the hurried humping of two desperate, sexually frustrated people.

So, I settled on taking the edge off for both of us, focusing on making Ashlyn feel good, knowing as pent up as I was it wouldn't take much to get me off anyway. And I'd been right—after caressing Ashlyn and feeling her curves against me, listening to the sweet sounds she made as I brought her to climax with my fingers—it had taken little more than a couple strokes of her hand to have me spending.

Then after we were both sated and exhausted, I carried her out of the tub, dried her off, and tucked her against me in bed. We'd fallen asleep quickly, both still naked, her soft, warm body draped across me.

I guess jerking off against Ashlyn hadn't quite calmed my raging lust as much as I'd hoped though, as I stirred awake several times in the night so hard and desperate, I'm surprised I didn't give in, rollover, and rut her like an animal.

It's no surprise I'd wake up this morning with a severe case of morning wood, but what *is* a surprise is opening my eyes to find Ashlyn with her lips wrapped around my rigid shaft.

The blankets are bunched around her luscious hips as she kneels between my spread legs. I push myself up onto my elbows and blink to clear the sleep from my eyes, as I watch the top of her head bob up and down, auburn hair fanning between us to tickle my lower abs.

Ashlyn fondles my balls and I groan, trying to clear my fogged brain that still can't comprehend what's happened.

Ashlyn Addison is in my bed, fully naked.

My princess is kneeling in front of me with my cock in her mouth and my balls in her hand.

"Fuck," I finally manage to rasp, my brain catching up at last to the present moment, and recalling the things she told me last night. "Princess, you don't have to do that. After what you said before…if you don't want to…"

Ashlyn releases my length with a wet pop, pushing the hair out of her face as she meets my gaze with sparkling hazel eyes, hands squeezing my thighs as she pushes up slightly.

"But I *do* want to Chase," she says, voice raw with desire.

"I've never seen a cock I *wanted* in my mouth, but yours…" She doesn't finish her statement before lowering her head, maintaining eye contact from below her long lashes as she licks me from root to tip, fisting the bottom part of my length before sucking as much of me down as she can.

"Shit," I sigh, letting my head fall back against the pillow as I brush the hair away from Ashlyn's face, so I can get a better look at what she's doing to me.

This is an image I never want to forget. It will fuel my fantasies whenever we're apart.

"Do you know how long I've wanted this, princess?" I groan as she takes me somehow deeper, gagging slightly as she slurps and sucks me down. "How many times I've imagined this exact moment? You look so fucking gorgeous with my cock in your mouth."

I can feel Ashlyn smile against me as she picks up the pace, and as much as I know I'd enjoy coming this way, that will have to wait for another time.

I want to release deep inside her, but not down her throat. I want to fill Ashlyn up until she overflows; let go of years and years of want for the right woman, for *this* woman, against her womb where I know my seed belongs.

So, I reluctantly pull Ashlyn up by the shoulders until she's straddling me, cup her cheeks, and kiss her hard, tasting her desire for me on her lips and tongue.

"I need you," I say as I pull away slightly, our breaths mingling together in the small space between our mouths. "I need to be inside you, here." I snake my hand down Ashlyn's body until I reach her center, parting her folds with a fingertip to run up and down her leaking slit. "You're already so wet for me, your body is *crying* for me, princess. Did you like sucking your man's big dick?"

Ashlyn nods and smiles temptingly. "I *loved* it, but now I want more. I want you inside me too." As though to emphasize her words, Ashlyn grabs the hand that is between her thighs and pushes two of my fingers inside her tight channel. We both moan at the feel of it.

"That's it," I say, thrusting my fingers into her harder. "Use my fingers to get yourself ready for me. You're so fucking *tight*. This pussy is going to feel so good squeezing my cock."

I thumb her clit as Ashlyn continues to fuck my hand, and soon I feel her clamp down on me as she comes, head rolling forward as she says my name over and over like a chant.

I remove my fingers from inside Ashlyn and give her a moment to recover, my stiff cock pulsing where it rests between her round ass cheeks, dripping and dying to get inside her.

"You ready for me now, princess?" I ask, tipping her chin up to meet my gaze.

She smiles. "So ready."

I lift her by the hips, gripping my cock by the base to line up with her entrance. "Go slow," I say as my head begins to part her lips. "Go as slow as you need, and then ride me when you want more."

I need Ashlyn completely in control. I have to do everything in my power to make sure this time is good for her—I want it to wipe out the memory of her painful past experiences.

If I hurt her, I'll die.

So, I let Ashlyn slowly lower herself onto me, taking my length inch by tortuous inch. I grab her round breasts in my hands, massaging them as she adjusts to my size and continues to sink lower, rocking her hips up and down along the way until finally, *finally*, she takes me to the hilt.

Ashlyn grabs my big biceps once I'm fully inside, and I drop my hands to her waist as she leverages my arms for balance, and begins to bounce up and down on my cock.

"Just like that," I groan, mesmerized by the place where we're joined, watching my long length disappear inside her with every sway of her hips. "Bounce and grind, go fast or slow. Do whatever feels good. Take what you need."

"Mm…" Ashlyn sighs, picking up her pace, rising and then bringing her core back down on me hard, the sound of our skin and the wet noises of our joining filling the room. The scent of cherry blossoms and sex is heavy in the air.

"All I need is you Chase," she continues, eyes locking with mine as she continues to move above me. "You're the only man who's ever made me come, and now I want you to be the only one to fill me up. I want all of you inside me."

"Yeah?" I say, one hand squeezing her waist while the other traces down and begins rubbing her clit. "Come again, princess. Come on my cock and I'll give you *everything*. Every last part of me."

Ashlyn whimpers at my words as I increase the pressure on her clit. It's not long before her thighs begin to jerk and her entire body tenses. When I feel her pussy pulse and then clench down on me, I know she's coming.

Ashlyn cries out and slumps forward, resting her forehead on my chest, but this time, I don't allow her to recover. I wrap my arms around her and swiftly roll until she's underneath me, my elbows resting on the pillow by her head as I hold myself above her, never breaking the connection of our bodies.

"Gonna fuck you now…*hard*," I say, already beginning to thrust in and out of her.

Ashlyn had the chance to go at her pace; to take her time, and now my patience is breaking.

I need to *rut*.

I need to spear her into the bed rough and deep. I want Ashlyn to feel me for *days*, for *weeks*.

When she leaves and goes back to California, I want there

to be no doubt who she belongs to. I need to imprint myself permanently upon her in the most primitive way.

I dip my face to her chest as I continue fucking Ashlyn ruthlessly. I find one dusky pink, perfect nipple and then the other with my lips and tongue, sucking at them until her back arches and her toes curl—lifting us both with the force of her pleasure.

"Oh my god, Chase!" Ashlyn cries as I piston inside, hitting her with long quick thrusts, making my headboard hit the wall with a *thump, thump, thump.*

"Gonna fill you up princess," I say as my balls draw up and my spine tingles, signaling the approach of my climax. "Gonna *drown* this pussy in me. Gonna give you all I have. Every drop."

"Yes, yes, *yes!*" I hear her cry out, coming again at the same time I release inside her. The walls of her hot channel grip and let go over and over as I spill into her womb, milking me until I'm completely empty.

I collapse on top of Ashlyn, forgetting how much bigger I am than her until she takes a shuddering breath beneath me.

"Sorry," I say as I begin to roll off, but Ashlyn isn't letting me go anywhere.

"No. Stay," she says, gripping me tightly to her chest, the softness of her tits against my skin threatening to make my cock stiffen once again. "I love the way you feel on top of me. The way you feel inside me. *Stay.*"

"Alright princess," I say, lifting onto my elbows, taking some of my weight off, and kissing her chastely on the lips. "Anything you want."

She sighs and we lay like that for a few moments, until Ashlyn speaks again, voice barely above a whisper.

"I never knew it could be like this. I never knew having a man inside me could feel like *everything*. I think...I think those other times don't count. They seem completely meaningless compared to this. You're my first, Chase. In all the ways that matter."

"Princess," I reply, kissing along her cheek to her ear. "I feel the same. Every past experience…those were all just sex. But this…this was making *love*."

* * *

WE FINALLY MAKE it out of bed about an hour later, and I cook Ashlyn breakfast. Ashlyn doesn't eat gluten or meat other than fish, but I just *happened* to have some plant-based bacon and gluten-free pancake mix on hand, along with my usual stock of eggs.

Ashlyn teased me for that, but I happily admitted that *yes*, I had hoped that maybe, just maybe, I'd get the chance to make her breakfast while she was here. So, I planned ahead.

We're finishing our food and coffee when my phone pings with a text. I look down and see a message from Javier.

> Hey. Wanted to let you know that the investigation is still ongoing, but none of Ashlyn's things from the fire are salvageable. Ella wants to bring her some clothes and anything else she needs. Figures she doesn't want to have to go out today after everything.

I show Ashlyn the message, and after some convincing, since she doesn't want to be a bother, I finally get her to send a message to Ella with more info on things she needs. As much as I enjoy seeing Ashlyn in my clothes, the baggy shirt she's wearing now revealing tantalizing glimpses of her creamy thighs, I know she'll be more comfortable with some things of her own—especially whenever we decide to leave my cabin.

While we wait for Ella, Ashlyn helps me clean up the

dishes from breakfast, even after I try telling her to just relax and let me handle it.

"You know I like doing things for myself, Chase," she says as she carries her plate to the sink, and then grabs the dirty pan off the stove to start scrubbing.

"I know," I reply, putting away the other leftover ingredients from the counter. "You're an independent woman. I get it," I tease and she snorts out a laugh. "You always make it a point to do things for yourself. Is that just because you don't like everyone always trying to wait on you, or is there some other reason?"

I've always known Ashlyn to be extremely self-sufficient, especially for someone who could pay, or hell, probably even have people *volunteer* to do everything for her. It's one of the qualities I like most about her, but we've never really talked about why she's that way. Especially considering she grew up in an extremely privileged family.

There is a lot about Ashlyn I still don't know.

"It's partly that," she responds, rinsing the pan and pulling the towel off the stove to dry it. "But it's mostly because of my dad. Even though I grew up in a famous family, he also never liked to be waited on. He preferred to do things for himself. Since I was always trying to gain his approval, I followed his example from an early age. Guess it stuck."

I nod. I know all about trying to win the approval of a parent.

"I get that," I say. "But that doesn't mean you have to face everything alone. You've got me now. You've also got Will and Flora, and Ella and Javier too. Plenty of people who care about you and are willing to help shoulder your problems. I'm glad you're letting us help you with the aftermath of the fire, I just wish you'd known how to accept support before now. Like with those men from your past. You should have told someone…"

I know I told Ashlyn last night I wouldn't talk about this again, but it's still eating at me—thinking about those Hollywood pieces of shit who took advantage of my girl.

She sighs. "I *did* tell someone, Chase." Ashlyn's voice is sad, and I immediately regret bringing it up, but I also know it's going to gnaw at me until I know more.

"You did?" I ask, unable to stop the anger evident in my voice. "Who did you tell? And why the hell didn't they do anything about it?" I'm clenching my fists now, ready to beat the life out of whoever let her down.

Ashlyn leaves the pan she's been cleaning in the sink and comes over to me. She takes my hand and squeezes it until I unclench my fist, and then entwines her fingers in my own. "It's okay, Chase," she soothes. "The man I told is dead. There's nothing you could do about it now anyway."

"I'd still like to know who you told."

Ashlyn sighs again and reluctantly answers. "My father. I told my father and he…he was so *ashamed* of me. He accused me of using my beauty and name to my advantage, and of not working hard enough…of taking the easy way out. He never liked that I wanted to be an actress anyway, so it made him more disappointed in me than he already was."

And just like that, I'm furious again. I'm ready to dig up the old man and send him right back to the grave.

"The easy way out?" I exclaim. "What happened to you was not *easy*, and it wasn't right. How could he think that of you? It's such…" I let my words go when Ashlyn squeezes my hand and looks up and me with tears in her sweet green-brown eyes.

"I know," Ashlyn raises my hand to her cheek and kisses my wrist as I cup her face. "I know that now, and I'm finally starting to let go of the misplaced guilt I have about what happened, and from how my dad made me feel about it after. But it's *hard*. That's why those memes and all the shit in the press about my dad being ashamed of me hurts so much. All I ever wanted to do was make him proud, and then he died before I could. And even now, I keep failing him. I might never get the type of role I want. I might never win an Oscar. And if I don't, then what's been the point of it all?"

"Princess," I reply, wiping the tears as they start to fall. "If your dad wasn't proud of you, then he was blind. You're a wonderful actress and a remarkable person. You work harder than anyone I've ever met, and you've sacrificed so much for your career. Don't sacrifice your soul, too. It's not worth it."

Ashlyn lets out a small sob and I wrap her in my arms, holding her close as she lets go of the pain I can tell she's been keeping inside for a long, long time.

"Would it help if I told you you're not alone when it comes to working yourself into the ground for a long-departed parent? I've spent years trying to make a dead man proud too."

As the words leave my mouth, I realize this is the deepest conversation Ashlyn and I have ever had. We've talked a bit about our family before—commiserating on both being only children, sharing about our father's deaths and my mother's sickness. But we've never drilled down below the surface, and I understand now that's what we have to do. We have to dig up all the parts of our pasts, the good and the bad, in order to build the foundation for our future.

A future I pray we'll live *together*.

Ashlyn sniffs into my shirt and raises her head from my chest.

"You have?"

I nod as I go on. "My dad was a doctor, and always wanted me to follow in his footsteps. But I was never that interested in medicine, and my grades weren't good enough anyway. It's not that I was stupid, it was just that school never seemed to hold my attention, and I spent much of my time there just trying to survive the bullies. I was always really tall, and until I finally started to get into sports and weightlifting at the end of high school, I was skinny and gawky. *'All knees and elbows,'* my mom would say. The other kids liked to pick on me and make my life hell, at least until I was strong enough to fight back. After that everyone was scared of me, so even when I wasn't being picked on, I never really had friends." I pause for a moment to look back down at Ashlyn, her eyes still hazed with tears. I brush a few off her cheeks as I continue.

"Anyway, I wasn't interested in going to college after I graduated, and my dad was crushed. He did his best not to show it, but his disappointment was obvious. I thought that when I found firefighting, an active profession I loved that helped save lives just like he did, that would be enough. But it wasn't. So, I became a paramedic too, hoping *that*, at long last, would make my dad proud. I'd just moved here to Hideaway to finish my training on the job at the fire district when my dad had a massive stroke. He passed away before I could make it back down to Denver. He died ashamed of his only son. The entire reason I took the job as chief was so that I could make him proud, even though he wasn't alive to see it and my mom had already forgotten me."

Ashlyn pulls back from me as I finish, blinking away tears and rising on her tiptoes to smooth her soft hands over my bristly face.

"Oh Chase," she says, "I'm so sorry. I never went to a proper school, so I can't imagine what it must have been like to be tormented by other kids. But I can understand the way you feel about your dad, and just like you told me, if your dad wasn't proud of you then he was a fool. You're amazing at what you do. You've saved lives and stopped homes from burning down. Think of Flora. If you hadn't been there to pull her out of that flooded car when she was just a baby, she wouldn't be here now, and can you imagine what a huge hole that would have left in so many lives? I bet if your dad could see you now, see the incredible man you've become, he would burst he'd be so proud."

My face cracks into a small smile. "I think your dad would be too, and even if not, even if neither of our fathers could ever be proud of the people we've become, it doesn't matter, does it? We have plenty of people who *do* value us, and most importantly, we have each other. I think it's time we start living for ourselves, and doing what we want to do, don't you?"

Ashlyn nods in agreement and kisses me softly.

"You know, for the record, I don't think you'd have made a good doctor, anyway. You're much too stern and grumpy. You'd have a terrible bedside manner," Ashlyn teases, lightening the heavy mood.

I laugh. "I think you're right. And have you seen my hands?" I say self-deprecatingly, raising my arm between us. "Can you imagine these sausage fingers performing surgery? No patient would survive."

Ashlyn giggles and takes my hand, making a show of inspecting it, rubbing her fingers over my calluses and turning it this way and that.

"Well," she says, "maybe these fingers weren't made to perform surgery, but I can think of a few other things they're *perfect* for."

"Is that right?" I say, lifting Ashlyn by the ass and planting her on the counter in front of me, pushing her legs wide with my big body. "Why don't you show me then, princess? Show me what these fingers are good for."

Ashlyn's eyes fill with need and she bites her plush lower lip. "Chase…" her voice is husky, "we shouldn't. Ella could be here at any…"

I don't let Ashlyn finish her statement before my hand shoots beneath the hem of the shirt she's wearing, cupping her bare pussy with my big palm.

Ashlyn moans and relaxes against my hand as I proceed to demonstrate *precisely* what my big fingers are good for.

ASHLYN

I'm in a deep sleep when I feel an unfamiliar sensation between my legs.

There's something hot and wet moving up and down my core, licking inside and then circling and sucking at my clit. I'm flushed and writhing as I slowly come awake, rubbing my eyes open to find a dark head just visible under the covers. I grip the edge of the blanket and lower it to find Chase situated within my spread thighs, navy eyes finding mine as I take him in.

Chase has turned the tables on me from yesterday morning, and I must say I was definitely on to something. This is a perfect way to wake up.

"Morning princess," Chase says, lips moving against my most sensitive place as he speaks, eyes wicked with want.

"Mmph," I sigh and let my head fall back, still half asleep and too turned on to form coherent words.

I didn't think being with Chase could get any better after yesterday, but this is a side of heaven I've yet to experience.

Chase's mouth on me there is...*delicious*.

We've both been insatiable since finally admitting our feelings, unable to keep our hands to ourselves. It's as though the past year has been one long, tortuous round of foreplay—seeing each other on video and talking almost daily, but unable to touch.

Now that we can it's almost all we've done. We spent some of yesterday talking, sharing deeper parts of our pasts we hadn't yet explored, connecting on a new level over our shared experiences with our fathers.

Our bodies were also pulled apart briefly when Will and Flora called to check in after hearing about the fire, and then when Ella and Javier came by to bring me some clothes and toiletries to replace what I'd lost—also delivering back the rental car Beau had taken to the inn. I guess he'd gotten a ride to the airport from a new bartender at the pub.

But as soon as I thanked Ella and Javier profusely for everything they'd done for me, making tentative plans for dinner in a few days, and they left; Chase and I had been right back at it. I needed him inside of me so badly and so often we started skipping foreplay altogether. He has no more problem getting hard than I have getting wet.

It's like we needed to keep coming together, quickly and frequently, to feel whole.

Somehow amid all that lovemaking, we skipped over this, and since I'd never been licked there before, I hadn't even thought of it.

And dear god I had no idea what I'd been missing. Chase's tongue is pure magic.

"Can't believe I waited so long to taste you," Chase groans between licks. "You're sweet and so fucking *sinful*."

He applies light suction with his lips as his tongue continues to work me, and I want *more*.

Mostly, I want to pleasure him again too. I'm addicted to us getting off together.

"Feels so good…" I moan. "But I want to taste you too."

Chase pauses and looks up, chin and cheeks shiny with my desire. "Okay," he says, that naughty grin back on his face as he slides up my body, kissing me once before flopping over beside me. "Come ride my face then, princess."

I hesitate briefly because I've never done this. The 69 position always seemed strange to me, but with Chase, I think I see the appeal. I can suck him off while he continues to lick me. More mutual pleasure. I can please him while he's pleasing me.

Feeling more confident I roll and turn, placing my knees on either side of Chase's head, hovering my drenched sex right above his lips. He growls and grabs my bottom with both hands, pulling me down, tracing his thumbs between my cheeks, and parting my swollen lips. He licks me from ass to clit before sucking the bundle of nerves back between his lips.

I groan and start rubbing myself all over his face, but then I remember I have a job to do too. I run my hands down his hard chest, smoothing my fingertips across the tattoo near his ribs, and then over his defined abs until they arrive at the base of his cock.

I grip him with one hand while the other strokes up his length, rubbing my thumb over the tip and precum dripping from the slit, lubricating my motions.

Chase groans and curses against my pussy when I lick him up like a popsicle and then suck him into my mouth, his words vibrating my clit and making me grind down harder on his mouth.

Chase feels heavy on my tongue as I slide it over him, licking up more of his arousal and marveling at the salty, masculine taste. I've never enjoyed a man's flavor before, but with Chase like everything else, it's different. I could suck his cock and drink him down daily and never mind it.

Not at all.

I close my lips tight around him and bob my head to the rhythm Chase is setting with his hips. I can feel his pulse in my mouth and see his balls draw up slightly, right as he plunges his tongue inside my sodden hole and then drags the tip back to my clit, inserting one finger into my channel.

He sucks hard and fast as my orgasm slams into me. I cry out with his cock halfway down my throat, and the sensation must be enough to set him off too, as I feel him swell and then release hot, salty jets in my mouth. I swallow it all down as my body melts into him, my climax making my thighs quiver and the blood rush to my ears. I can feel Chase groaning beneath me but I can't hear anything besides the beating of my own heart.

That was...*incredible.* My entire body feels like it's been blown apart. I'm surprised there aren't pieces of me splashed across the walls and ceiling.

After our breathing has calmed down, I finally roll off of him and turn my body so we're again face to face.

Chase looks at me with heavy lids, licking his lips and wiping my juices off his mouth with the back of his hand.

"No one's ever done that to me before," I remark. "I never even thought about it much before. But now...*fuck.* You may have created a monster. I might need you to lick me every day."

Chase smirks and chuckles, hand coming to caress my face.

"You might kill me, princess," he replies. "But what a way to go."

I laugh and scoot closer, kissing up his shoulder playfully before placing a quick peck on his lips.

"Well, I guess I should give you a little break," I say, sitting up and moving towards the side of the bed. "I'm going to take a shower. Unless...you want to join me?"

Chase groans and shakes his head. "You forget I'm an old man. As much as I'd like to, I think I may need my rest. I've got *plans* for you later, you see."

I giggle and swat his arm before I climb out of bed and head to the bathroom.

I shower, taking my time washing my hair and letting the hot water relax my pleasantly sore muscles, and then head to the closet attached to the en suite, throwing on a light pink maxi dress that Ella brought me.

When I head back out to the bedroom, I expect to see Chase still in bed, maybe even asleep. Instead, he's dressed in jeans and a gray Hideaway Valley Fire District T-shirt, standing by the window, looking out towards the pine trees and golden aspen that surround his cabin.

I can only see his profile, but his jaw looks tense.

What happened to the playful man I left in bed?

"Chase," I say, moving closer to him. "Is something wrong?"

He turns and holds my phone out to me. "Your agent called."

"Oh," I reply. I hadn't told her that I'd left or where I was going, so I knew it would only be a matter of time before she'd check in. "Did you answer it?"

He nods. "I wasn't sure if it might be important. She called and I let it go to voicemail the first time, but then she called again so I picked up. I guess that director you worked with before, the one that kissed you and the paparazzi caught on film, was just arrested. Several women came out with sexual assault allegations. She wanted to let you know in case you had anything you needed to report. She also said that she'd spoken with someone inside the Academy about your Oscar nomination. I guess word had gotten out to some about the director being under investigation, and your snub was more about not wanting to nominate any of his work. It didn't have anything to do with you."

I nod and sigh. It's a relief in more ways than one.

"That's good," I reply. "But he didn't try anything more with me after that kiss. I knew he was a womanizer but I'd never heard about any assault allegations. I'm glad they've arrested him if that's the case."

Chase nods and releases a long breath, and I expect him to relax after this revelation, assuming he must have been worried that my former director had hurt me too. But now he looks more tense than ever.

"That's not all," he goes on. "She also said that you'd been offered a role. I guess it's a modern remake of *Pride and Prejudice*, and they want you to play Elizabeth Bennet."

My face goes slack with shock. That's my all-time favorite book and *dream role.*

Cliché though it may be since many actresses want to play the witty and independent Miss Bennet, it's always been the one part I wanted more than any other.

Chase knows this too. I've told him.

So why does he look so pissed about it?

He continues and it becomes clear.

"The movie starts filming in six weeks, and they want you there in two. I guess the original actress who got the part had to quit at the last minute for some reason. I told your agent I'd let you know, and they need a decision by tomorrow."

Chase is glaring at me, and I can see in his cold blue eyes exactly what he thinks.

He thinks I'm going to drop everything, *drop him,* to take the part.

That's not fair. He's making assumptions without even hearing me out.

He's right that I'm not going to downright refuse it, as it's everything I've ever worked for. But he still shouldn't think

I'd take it without any thought to how it would impact him and our future together.

"And you think I'm going to take it and just *leave*?" I say, trying to suppress the anger filling my chest.

"Aren't you?" Chase replies flatly.

"Do you really think after everything that's happened between us, everything we've shared, that I'd take off without even a discussion with you?"

"It's the part you've always wanted. So, *take it*. I know that's what you want to do. Take it and leave, and we can go back to talking over Facetime and never being in the same room or state or even *country*." Chase has raised his voice slightly, he's not yelling, but he's obviously upset.

"Okay," I say, voice raising to meet his. "What exactly are my other options, Chase? To not take it and just stay here with you forever? Why should *I* have to be the one to give up all my dreams? You could quit your job and come with me."

Chase shakes his head and takes a step closer to me, jaw still tensed. "I'd happily give up *everything* for you, Ashlyn," he says. "I love you and I'd follow you anywhere if I thought we would truly be *together* if I did. If I go with you, you'll just work and work and *work* and I'll barely see you. I want more than that. I want *you. All of you.* I want a house together, kids, and a stable life and family. I'm sick of waiting."

I take a breath to calm my nerves before I say something I'll regret. Part of me can tell Chase just has his defenses up, that he's afraid I'll leave him so he's brisling and coming at me in an attempt to keep himself from being hurt, and I consider saying that. But I can tell by the look on his face he isn't ready to hear it.

The man just told me *he loves me* for the first time in the worst possible way, for Christ's sake. He isn't thinking straight.

"Chase," I reply, trying to keep my voice even. "I love you

too, and no matter what decision I make or how far apart we are, nothing will ever change that. But I have to think about this, okay? I can't just make a decision this big based purely on emotion."

He frowns and doesn't respond, turning back to the window.

"Maybe we need a bit of time…apart," I say reluctantly, grabbing my phone off the nightstand, and opening it to my group text with Will and Flora. "This has all happened so fast, and been so intense, with the fire and…and *everything*. Maybe I can go see Flora and Will for a while, and talk to them about it. The time alone in the car might be good for me to just…*think*. It will give us both a chance to think and give you a chance to cool down."

Part of me expects, and hopes he'll protest. He'll say he's being an ass and that we'll figure it out together, but he doesn't.

Chase just keeps standing there, not looking at me and nods his head.

I punch in a quick text to Flora and Will. Will responds right away saying they're home and I'm welcome to come over.

"Will said I can head over," I say, taking a step towards Chase, and putting a hand on his large forearm, giving the sold muscle a little reassuring squeeze. "I'm going to go now, and I'll text you when I get there. I'll see you soon, and we'll talk more, okay?"

He just nods again, still not looking at me.

I've seen glimpses of this side of Chase before, a side that shuts down emotion and avoids hard conversations, but I've never seen it like *this*.

I know he's afraid.

I am too.

Neither of us wants to lose the other.

I just hope we can find a way forward together.

* * *

A FEW MINUTES later I'm driving up the winding mountain road, grateful that I'd inputted the directions into my phone before I left Chase's and lost service. I couldn't figure out how to get the stupid blue tooth in the rental car to connect to my phone, so I gave up and just put it on the center console with the volume cranked up. The route seems pretty straight forward and I kind of remember it, but I drive so rarely I didn't want to risk getting lost.

I'm realizing now just how out of practice I am as I navigate the curvy mountain roads. So, I slow down to a crawl and hope if someone comes up behind me there won't be anyone approaching in the opposite direction and they can go around.

I'm about ten minutes in when I start to feel tears burning my eyes again. It had taken everything in me, every last piece of my fractured pride, not to break down in front of Chase. Not that he would have seen, as he continued to avoid looking at me as I prepared to leave, and didn't even follow me out of the bedroom to say goodbye.

I've been holding my sobs in—pushing them back down every time they try and creep to the surface, reassuring myself everything will be fine.

I'll talk to Flora and Will, and get their advice (Flora's known Chase forever so I know she'll have helpful insights), and I'm certain by the time I head back down the mountain Chase will be seeing things more objectively. Then we'll talk and figure out a plan that will work for both of us.

I'm sure of it.

I keep repeating this to myself as I drive, and I'm so distracted I don't notice the truck coming up quickly behind me until it's right on my tail. At first, I speed up, but then the road curves and I have to slow back down.

I take a breath as the truck gets closer and look over into the other lane. We're on a broken yellow line, and there are no other cars on the road, so surely whoever it is will just go around me.

But they don't, and a moment later I hear a loud thud at the same time my car lurches forward, the truck ramming my bumper. I scream and grip the wheel as the tires jerk, trying to regain control. For a moment I do, but then the truck hits me again from behind, harder, causing me to swerve off the road.

My front tire hits a larger boulder, and I hear the crunching of metal as I'm thrown slightly forward and my car comes to a stop. Luckily, I wasn't going that fast so the airbags don't deploy, and I'm shaken but not hurt.

I don't have time to try and see if the vehicle is still drivable before the truck pulls up behind me, and a man slowly gets out. He's average height and build, dressed in black, and looks to be in his early twenties.

There's something in his hand too, and I can't be sure since my mind is in full-on flight or fight mode and my eyesight is hazy with adrenaline, but I think it's a *gun*.

My stomach falls and panic sets in, because I know *exactly* who it is. With everything else going on he'd barely even crossed my mind since the fire. Even though I've never seen his face before, I know without a doubt it's *him*.

My stalker.

Eternally Yours.

As he gets closer, I make a split-second decision—my addled brain and twitching body determining *flight* to be the most likely means of escape.

And maybe it's a stupid choice since if he *is* carrying a gun, he's more than close enough to fatally shoot me, but I'm past the point of logical thought.

So, before my stalker can reach me, I fly into action.

I throw open my door and *run.*

CHASE

The moment Ashlyn leaves I realize what a complete ass I'm being.

But that phone call from her agent sent me down to a dark place inside—a place that reminded me our time together has an expiration date.

Even if she hadn't been offered this part now, eventually she would be offered a new role, her career would be back on track, and she'd have no reason to stay here with me.

It's not like I have all that much to offer her. She's a beautiful, talented woman, and I'm just a grumpy small-town fire chief. I've never been good enough for anyone else, not even my parents, so why would I be good enough for her?

I thought we'd have more time together before reality came crashing down though, throwing me out of this perfect dream I've created with Ashlyn the past two days.

We hadn't talked about our future yet, or what would happen once her vacation was over, so I knew we'd have to discuss it eventually. But when that call came today, I wasn't prepared.

I wasn't ready to let her go yet, and instead of telling her that, telling her I didn't want to lose her, instead I acted like a complete *dick*.

In trying to hold her here, I instead only managed to push her away.

Sure, Ashlyn had been patient and barely raised her voice in response to my behavior—even though she had every right to—and tried to reassure me before she left, but that doesn't mean I didn't just completely, *irreversibly*, fuck everything up.

Did I also really tell her that I love her, for the first time, during an *argument*?

Shit.

Not only that, but I also let Ashlyn leave by herself, even though I promised her and Beau—who'd been reluctant to step away from his role as her protector—that I would be her bodyguard while she was in Hideaway.

It may only be a twenty-minute drive, and I know Ashlyn said she wanted some time to herself, but I still should never have let her go alone. I was so deep in my head and damn fool emotions that the risk didn't occur to me.

I also didn't even tell her goodbye.

Fuck!

I think I've got some serious groveling to do.

I'm ready to beg Ashlyn to come back as soon as she texts me that she's arrived safely at Flora and Will's, but the text never comes.

I wait another ten minutes past when she should have arrived, and then I call Will.

Maybe she's angrier than she let on and decided not to text when she got there, but that isn't like her at all.

There's a sinking feeling in my stomach, and my heart starts to pound as I wait for Will to pick up.

Something isn't right.

"Chase," Will says, picking up on the third ring. "Flora was just getting ready to call you. Ashlyn should have been here by now, but she isn't answering her phone. She might just be in a spot without service, but we're worried she may be lost."

"I never should have let her go alone," I grumble, but this is not the time to beat myself up. Ashlyn is out there somewhere on this mountain, and we need to find her. "I'll head out now and look for her. Can you or Flora call Javier, and have him get the search and rescue team out?"

Search and rescue works under the purview of the fire district, and even though someone usually needs to be missing longer for them to be deployed, I know Javier will understand the urgency of the situation.

I'm ready for Will to tell me I'm overreacting—already wanting to get emergency services involved, but he must sense that something is wrong too, as he readily agrees.

"I'll have Flora call Javier and the police as well, just in case. I'm going to head out and try to find her now too."

"Good," I reply. "I'll have my satellite phone with me, and make sure to take yours as well in case we don't have service. Be in touch if you hear anything and I'll do the same."

As a remote mountain firefighter, I carry a satellite phone for my job, and I know Flora, an avid outdoorswoman who grew up in Hideaway, keeps one for emergencies as well.

"Sounds good," Will says before hanging up.

With that, I spring into action. My satellite phone is already in my truck, but there is one other thing I grab before I head out the door.

My gun.

I hope I don't need it, but I intend to be ready if I do.

I wouldn't hesitate for a moment to kill anyone who threatened the life of my princess.

***

I make it halfway up the mountain when I see a truck pulled off awkwardly to the side of the road. I slow down, and as I begin to pass it, I see Ashlyn's SUV several yards ahead, its front tire and bumper smashed firmly into a boulder. Both vehicles appear to be empty.

This is bad.

My heart starts to race and my entire body starts to shake as it fills with adrenaline. I take a few breaths to calm myself as I park in front of Ashlyn's car, knowing I need to keep a clear head for this.

I'm a trained firefighter and medic for fuck's sake. I'm not about to start panicking when the woman I love needs me the most.

I take a few more deep breaths and then get out of my truck, grabbing my satellite phone and securing my gun in its holster around my waist, hidden below my shirt.

I'm trained to track people lost in the mountains, so I start by examining the scene for traces of what might have happened, and where Ashlyn and the owner of the other vehicle may have gone.

I walk to the truck first, noticing a few scraps on the front bumper. The driver-side door is unlocked, so I take a look inside but the cab appears to be empty, and I don't have time to investigate it further. Instead, I close the door and start to approach Ashlyn's car from the rear, noticing dents on the back bumper that seem to correspond to the ones on the truck.

This asshole ran her off the road!

I suppress my building rage as I approach the open door to her car. Her purse is still on the passenger seat, and her phone is abandoned in the console.

I grab it and put it in my back pocket, then look at the

ground beneath me for signs of struggle or footprints indicating where she may have gone.

I see one set of small prints in the dirt that look to be from the flip-flops she was wearing, starting from below the driver's side door and then moving around into the trees on the other side of the car. Near those I see a set of larger footprints, appearing to be from boots, following behind and on top of the smaller ones.

I pull out my phone as I start to follow the trail, placing a call to the Chief of the Hideaway Valley Police District.

He answers on the first ring.

"Sam," I say, "Did you talk to Javier or Flora? Did they tell you about the situation with Ashlyn?"

Sam is an old-timer in Hideaway, and getting ready to retire. Javier and I work with him and the rest of the police force regularly, and he, like many others in town, has known Flora all her life.

"Yeah," he says. "Search and rescue are already out, and I've got guys ready to go if needed. Do you have news?"

"I do," I say as I move into the tree line, continuing to watch the two sets of prints below my big boots. They aren't visible everywhere, as some terrain is rockier and more compact than other areas. So, when I can't see them clearly, I look for other signs someone has gone by—like broken or bent tree branches or trampled vegetation. There isn't a formal hiking trail here, but there are a few different paths worn into the mountainside by both people and animals.

"I found Ashlyn's car along with another one pulled to the side of the Valley Highway, near mile marker 12. It looks like whoever was in the truck ran Ashlyn off the road, and I'm following two sets of prints into the woods now."

"Mile marker 12," Sam replies, and I hear him jotting down notes. "I'll send my guys and get word over to Javier's team, and Will too since I know he's out looking also. And

Chase," he says gruffly in a fatherly way; like a man preparing to advise a son he knows isn't going to listen. "You really shouldn't follow on foot by yourself. We'll have a team up there in no time. You should stay put and wait for help."

"I'm armed," I grunt, and I hear Sam sigh.

"Yeah, I figured. I had to at least try to stop you though. Stay in touch if you find anything else, and I'll be in contact soon. Be careful."

"I will. Be sure to remind your guys to keep quiet about Ashlyn, too. We don't want the media getting ahold of this," I say. Sam agrees and I hang up. As I slide my phone back into my pocket, I notice the two sets of footprints in front of me separating. It looks like Ashlyn ran in one direction and her pursuer in the other.

Good girl, I think. She managed to lose him.

I start following Ashlyn's prints as I place a quick call back to Sam, letting him know the direction I'm headed and the way it looks like the person chasing her took.

Suddenly the prints stop, and I can't make out where they continue. I look around at the surrounding landscape, noticing a break in the trees where prairie grasses and wildflowers are growing. I notice a large gap between a few sunflowers and I go to it, finding Ashlyn's discarded flip-flops. They must have become too hard to run in once she decided to venture off the dirt trail.

I continue to follow the signs of flattened vegetation until I emerge on another haphazard path. Here I see the faint impression of toes, so I follow them forward to a rock outcropping.

At this point, the trail becomes impossible to follow, since you can't leave footprints in granite. So, I climb up the boulders slowly, looking for any signs of life and letting my gut direct me.

Then, I hear a faint whisper from behind.

"Chase?"

I turn and follow the voice, and see a small hand emerge on the side of a large rockface. Part of Ashlyn's face emerges next, dripping with sweat and panic clear in her big eyes.

Ashlyn has managed to hide in the gap between two large boulders, so well disguised I didn't even see her or think to look.

I'm so proud of my princess. She's smart and knows how to take care of herself, but she shouldn't always have to. I know I should have been there for her, and prevented this from happening, but I'm relieved she was able to get away and hide on her own.

I move towards her and she grabs my hand, pulling me into the tight space with her.

There is barely enough room for us both, so we're touching from hips to chest.

"Princess," I say, cupping my hands around her beautiful face. "I'm so, so sorry. I never should have let you leave. I was such as fucking ass. Are you alight? Please tell me you're not hurt."

"It's okay," she whispers, golden-green eyes locking on mine. "I'm okay. I knew you'd find me. But we need to be quiet. A man is chasing me and I don't know where he is. I think he has a gun."

I shake my head. "I tracked you, and he went in the other direction. But even if he finds us, I'm here now. I won't let him touch you. I'll fucking *kill* him. I'll die before I let something happen to you."

"I know," she says, pushing up to kiss my lips softly. "But I still think it's best to stay hidden for now. I'd like to keep you alive." We both smile at each other weakly. I just found Ashlyn, and my life finally feels worth living—so *yeah*, I'd prefer to stay alive too.

"The police and search and rescue are all out looking for him, but it's probably best to stay put for now. I'll call and tell them I found you, but first, can you tell me exactly what happened?"

Ashlyn lets out a breath. "I was driving, and I noticed this truck getting close behind me. I thought he'd go around, but instead, he rammed me twice. I lost control and ended up crashing on the side of the road. When I saw him get out of the car, I knew it was him….*my stalker*. Then I saw he had a gun and I didn't even think, I just got out and ran. I'm faster than I realized I guess, because I lost him pretty quickly. Then I found these boulders and decided to hide. But I knew the entire time you'd find me. I *knew* it." Ashlyn digs her fingers into my shirt, scrapping my chest through the material, tears pooling in her eyes.

I blink as I take in her words, my mind catching on one statement in particular. "What do you mean, your *stalker*?"

Ashlyn sighs and buries her head under my chin. "I should have told you…I've been getting these notes and weird gifts from a stalker, Eternally Yours, for a few months now. I've had stalkers before and nothing ever came of it, so I guess I didn't think it was a big deal. Beau was handling it and I didn't want to worry you."

"Beau *knew*?" I reply, squeezing my hands where they've landed on her shoulders.

"Yes," she answers, looking back up at me. "But don't be mad at him. I made Beau promise not to tell you. If he'd thought there was any way my stalker would have found out I left California and followed me here, he would have told you. He would have made sure there was a whole team of security monitoring my every move."

I flex my jaw and again suppress the rage building inside me.

I'll deal with Beau later. For now, my priority is making sure Ashlyn is safe and catching the creep who's been following her.

I wiggle a bit to pull my phone from my pocket, my ass only a few inches from the rock face. I call Sam and let him know the situation, and he agrees we should stay where we are until a team can get to us.

"Have they found him yet?" Ashlyn asks when I hang up, keeping my phone in one hand for easy access.

"Not yet, but they will soon. We're going to stay here until the police get to us."

Ashlyn nods, rubbing her chin against my chest, her breath hot on my neck as she takes a deep breath, pressing herself tighter against me.

"I love you, Chase," she says, her lips brushing my skin as she talks. "That's all I could think about when I was running. That's all that matters to me. I love you, and I just want to be with you. I don't care about anything else."

I kiss the top of her head and speak into her soft auburn hair. "I love you too, princess. When I found your empty car...*shit*...I was so scared I'd never get to tell you that again, properly this time. I don't deserve you, but I love you too much to care. You're *mine*."

Ashlyn pulls away slightly, tipping her head up to look at me again. "You do *so* deserve me. My life was empty before you, all I did was focus on work, trying to distract myself from how lonely I was. But then I met you and that all changed. No one has ever cared about me the way you do. You're the first person in my entire life who has ever made me a priority. You were my best friend already, and now you're my lover too. I never dreamed I'd meet a man who loves me the way you do. So don't you *ever* think again, not for a second, that I'd give you up for some stupid part in a movie. I'm not going anywhere. Not without you. You're stuck with me now, Chase Morath."

I nod as I kiss her gently and squeeze her close.

Damn right.

Ashlyn's mine.

I'm hers.

And I'll never let her go again.

ASHLYN

I continue to hold tightly to Chase, pressed against his strong chest in our hiding place as we wait for the police to arrive.

There's nowhere in the world I'd rather be.

I was terrified as I ran from my stalker; images from my life flashing in front of my eyes while I tripped across dirt and over rocks, willing my body on when I wanted to stop, desperate to put as much distance as possible between myself and the man chasing me.

Through all the pictures and memories that floated through my mind as I continued to run, one person was ever-present: *Chase*. The moments I'd shared with him were the best, most meaningful of my life. I knew then that I wouldn't give him up for anything—not even the role I've always dreamed of.

Once I found my hiding place in between the boulders, I was finally able to slow my breathing and racing thoughts. As afraid as I still was, I also felt strangely at peace as I leaned on the rough rock, breathing in the comforting smell of spruce trees around me—the scent of the mountains so like Chase—spicy and warm and free.

My fear receded slightly at the thought, knowing Chase wouldn't stop until he found me. And when he did, I'd share with him a plan for our future that I think will make us both happy.

"Chase," I say, my face still burrowed into his chest, letting the calming sound of his beating heart soothe my remaining fears. "I think I have a way we can be together and both get what we want."

"Princess" he replies, his chest rumbling against my ear. "What I said earlier…I was being a complete idiot. Though I do want kids and a family, all I need is you. I was so afraid you were going to leave me that I lost my head. Forgive me, sweetheart. I'll quit my job and go with you to Antarctica if that's what you want. As long as we're together, I'll be happy. Your happiness is my happiness."

I giggle a little—only Chase could make me laugh at a time like this. "I have no intention of going to Antarctica," I start, "and I won't be happy unless you're happy too. If I talk to my agent and the role sounds like a good fit, you could come with me on location. Then, when it wraps, we'll come home, here to Hideaway. I'll take a hiatus, and we'll start a family. That's what I want too."

Chase sighs and pulls me tighter by the hips, even though we're already as close as two people can be.

"You sure? You won't miss your life in California?"

I shake my head and look up at him, seeing all the love I have for him reflected in his navy eyes.

"I never liked my life in Hollywood, not really. Everyone I care about, all my real friends, are here anyway. This feels like home. *You* feel like home." I lift on my tiptoes to kiss him tenderly, and before it can turn into something more heated, we're interrupted by the buzzing of Chase's phone.

It vibrates into my hipbone where Chase still holds it in his hand, pressed against me.

"Do you have good news for me, Sam?" Chase says as he answers, and we're close enough that I can hear the man on the other side of the line.

"I do. We caught him. He came back to his truck where my men were waiting. The gun was fake, and he's already singing like an opera star on opening night—telling us he never meant to hurt Ashlyn, that he loves her. He certainly seems obsessed and not right in the head. It sounds like he might have been responsible for the fire too."

"Do you have a name?" Chase grinds out, anger evident in his tone.

"Not yet, so cool your jets before you go planning his murder. He's just a kid, Chase. A *sick* kid it would seem. Can't be much over 20."

"That's old enough. I can't believe that fucking sicko…" I grab Chase's big, tattooed bicep and squeeze.

"They've got him, Chase," I say. "Let the police do their job."

"Listen to your girl, Morath," the voice on the other end agrees. Chase grumbles but drops it, then tells Sam to send whoever was coming to us back—that he can take care of me from here.

I do not doubt that.

In fact, I'm hoping…

I squeeze out from between the rocks, pulling Chase with me. Once we're both out in the open, I fly at him, climbing the man like a tree.

The way I've always wanted to.

He chuckles in surprise as I wrap my arms around his neck and my legs around his waist, my flowy, dirt-stained dress bunching up between us. I rock my hips as I kiss him fiercely, something long and hard pressing against my thigh.

"Is that a gun in your pocket or are you just happy to see me?" I joke, pulling my lips from his.

"Actually," Chase replies, carrying me over to a large rock and setting me down. Then he lifts his shirt to reveal a gun strapped to his hip.

I gasp as he takes it off, putting it on the ground.

Maybe I'm a little...*twisted,* but knowing that Chase was willing to *kill* to protect me is a major turn-on.

My pussy is already growing wet, arousal soaking my panties as Chase walks back to me. All the fear and adrenaline and *relief* mixing to make my need for him more intense than ever before.

Chase sinks to his knees in front of me and begins to gather my skirt and pull it up my thighs. He pushes my legs apart with his impossibly broad shoulders, hands running up my hips, ribs, and then cupping my breasts over the material of my dress, eyes locking on mine.

"I think I have some groveling to do," Chase says, rubbing his thumbs over my beaded nipples. "I need to make up for chasing you away earlier, don't you think?"

I nod. I like where this is going. This is shaping up to be the best apology I've ever received.

Chase smiles in that wicked way of his, hands dipping under my dress to grab my panties and pull them off, the material sticking for a moment over my dripping center before peeling away.

He shoves my underwear in his back pocket, before lowering his head between my legs. Big, rough hands run up the sensitive skin of my inner thighs as he breathes in my desire.

"This pussy is more soaked than ever," Chase says, running one finger up and down my seam.

I nod. I can feel the wetness dripping from my hole and running over my ass cheeks. "Look at what a mess you're making. Do you want your man to clean you up, princess? Show you how sorry I am with my lips and tongue?"

"Yes," I moan, grabbing the back of his head and pulling him towards my aching core. "Lick me like a good boy, and maybe I'll think about forgiving you."

Chase laughs and goes willingly. He stiffens his tongue to tease over my engorged clit, then latches onto me with his lips. He laves me with fast strokes as his fingers trace from my thighs, over my stomach, and up to my breasts.

I push myself into his big palms and cover his heavily veined hands with my own as I grind my pussy against his mouth. My thighs begin to jerk around his head, the familiar tingle spreading out from my center. But, before I can climax, Chase stands up.

I whimper at his sudden departure, but when I see the desperation in his dark eyes, pupils blown wide, I understand.

"Need to be inside you," he says, taking my hands and moving them to the button of his jeans, my face level with his huge bulge. "Take me out, princess. I want to see your hands on my big cock."

I bite my lower lip, willing my worked-up body to steady enough so I can work the fly of his jeans. Once they open I shove them and his underwear roughly down his thighs, closing my hands around his length, marveling at how my fingers don't quite encircle him.

I can feel his pulse beating beneath my palm as I stroke him from root to tip, spreading a bead of moisture over the broad head with my thumb.

Chase shivers.

I'm getting ready to put him in my mouth when he suddenly kneels and scoops me into his arms, shuffling a few steps to the side so he can rest my back against the rock face.

I bury my face in Chase's neck as he lines us up, breathing

in the scent of pine and sweat, licking the saltiness off his skin before nipping gently.

"Fuck!" Chase groans as he spears into me, rocking in and out a few times before pushing back to look at me.

"Keep your eyes on me, princess," he says as he picks up the pace, thrusting into my tight heat harder and harder. The rough granite behind me is scrapping at my skin every time he pounds into me, but I don't care. The pleasure between my thighs is too intense for me to feel anything else.

I lock eyes with Chase, connecting with him in a way I never have before. This man is my protector, my lover, my future husband.

Chase is my life.

"I love you," I say, happy tears filling my eyes. "You saved me, Chase. You saved my life."

And he did.

Not just today, when he rescued me from my stalker. Chase saved me that day a year ago when we first met; the day he made me a priority in his life. I was a shell of a person before that, moving through the motions of my life without any real care or purpose.

He changed that. Filled my life with the love I've always wanted and never had.

"You saved me too, princess," Chase replies, and I know exactly what he means.

We saved each other from a life of loneliness, from thinking we were unworthy of love. In loving each other, we've also learned to love ourselves.

"You're my whole heart, Ashlyn. I love you."

I continue to stare into Chase's eyes, both hands locked around his nape as his thrusts become punishing—the sounds of our joining and each broken moan echoing off the rock walls surrounding us.

I'm completely cracked open as he fills me so deep I could

burst, the tip of his cock hitting a place inside that makes my entire body start to tremble.

I chase the feeling, pumping my hips to meet his every movement, the intensity building and building until *finally*, at long last, I break apart.

My gaze never wavers from Chase as the orgasm rushes through me, my body trembling with pleasure.

"You look so fucking pretty when you come on my cock," Chase groans, hitting me with several more thrusts before I feel him swell and spill wet heat inside me, my inner walls still fluttering with the remnants of release, forcing out every drop he has to give.

We kiss tenderly, hearts beating together as we come down from the heights.

"I think it's time to take you home," Chase says a few minutes later, lowering me back down until my bare feet hit the dirt underneath us.

I'd almost forgotten that I'd kicked off my shoes when running earlier. I'm still surprised I was able to move so quickly in flip-flops and a long dress, one hand holding up the skirt as I maneuvered between rocks and trees.

I shake a little at the memory, recalling how close I came to losing everything.

"You okay, princess?" Chase asks, feeling me quiver in his arms.

"I'm fine. I'm perfect, actually," I say, emphasizing my statement with a kiss.

Chase smiles. He puts his gun back in place around his hips and then lifts me into his arms.

I consider protesting, his intention to carry me back to his truck clear. But I know it won't do any good, so I settle myself against him as he starts to move, wrapping my arms around his thick neck.

"Let's go, princess," Chase says. "After all that, you need rest. Maybe a bath."

I love the way he takes care of me, so I don't argue—even though he's wrong.

I don't need any of those things.

All I need is this man—this stern, sweet, protective man.

My Chase.

Everything I need, for the rest of my life, is already right here in my arms.

EPILOGUE

SIX MONTHS LATER

Chase

Ashlyn looks so beautiful walking down the aisle that for a moment, I forget to breathe.

The dress she wears is tight over her growing stomach, swelling as our baby girl grows. Ashlyn has always been the most gorgeous woman I've ever known, but now that's she pregnant with *my* child, she's somehow even lovelier.

As Ashlyn gets closer to where I stand, she turns and takes her place next to Flora.

No—this isn't *our* wedding or a wedding at all. Yet. We're at the rehearsal for Ella and Javier's wedding, which will be taking place tomorrow.

Ashlyn and I were married almost six months ago, shortly before we left for London. Ashlyn took the part of Elizabeth Bennet, with the stipulation she wouldn't come to set for three weeks (so we could plan a small ceremony and I could have time to pass the torch of fire chief to Javier). She also had a break for the holidays in December written into her contract, so we could come back to Hideaway and spend the season with the people we love and who've become our family.

We were married at the Hideaway Inn, which was fitting since that was where we first met. Flora shut the place down for the day, and the only people in attendance were her, Will, Callum (Flora's cousin and manager of the pub) his new wife Analise, Javier, and Ella.

Something changed between Javier and Ella that day, as they watched Ashlyn and I declare our love for each other. I'm not sure exactly what happened, but whatever it was, the next time I spoke to Javier he asked my advice on how to win her.

Shortly after we arrived in the U.K., Ashlyn and I spoke with Sam, who'd been working with the FBI to investigate and prosecute Ashlyn's stalker.

We learned his name was Scott Shultz, a tech genius only a few years out of high school. The kid had somehow managed to hack into almost every part of Ashlyn's life, including her phone, computer, and security system, which is how he was able to leave his gifts without ever showing up as more than a blur on camera.

Scott learned Ashlyn was coming to Colorado through her text messages, so he followed her and hacked into the security of her rental property too. He then snuck into the house and started a fire (which he cleverly disguised as originating from an electrical panel), to flush Ashlyn out to where he was waiting. Apparently, he hadn't accounted for the fact that Beau was still there, or for how quickly emergency response would arrive—impeding his plans and making it impossible for him to kidnap her.

After the fire, Scott continued to track Ashlyn through her phone, where he learned she was staying with me. The kid was smart enough to realize I'd have likely killed him if he tried to take her from my cabin, so he watched and waited for his opportunity to strike—which came when Ashlyn left by herself to go to Flora and Will's.

Once Scott was caught, he admitted to everything quickly, all the while swearing his love for Ashlyn and that he never intended to hurt her. During the investigation, it also came out that the kid had a long history of untreated mental health issues that had been long ignored by his parents. Because of that, Ashlyn asked the prosecution to consider treatment for Scott's illnesses instead of prison time.

The protective part of me, the merciless, lizard-brained side, wanted to argue against this—wanted to lock the fucker up and throw away the key. But it was Ashlyn's decision to make, not mine, and once I tried to look at the situation more objectively, I could see that she was right. Scott ended up making a plea deal stipulating mandatory mental health treatment and is now safely away from the public getting the help he needs.

When we arrived back in Hideaway in February to begin Ashlyn's hiatus from acting, it was a relief to know we could leave the whole ordeal behind us, especially since we'd found out in January that we were going to be parents sooner than we'd anticipated. It was lucky Ashlyn wrapped filming before she started showing, as she's now nearly 18 weeks along.

I enjoyed my time in London more than I thought I would—having never really left Colorado. Ashlyn loved showing me everything, especially when we visited a rocky beach and I saw the ocean for the first time in my life.

But I'm glad to be back here now, home with the woman I love and the other most important people in my life.

I smile at Ashlyn and then look around the rest of the

space, full of our found family. We're all gathered in an old restored farmhouse that sits on the property of the first (and hopefully only) resort in Hideaway Mountain. The larger resort isn't open yet, but the refurbished old house which includes a bar, restaurant, and several rooms for lodgers, has opened its doors early for the event.

There have been an abundance of new couples and marriages in Hideaway recently, but Ella and Javier's wedding is by far the largest. Ella, who helps manage the Hideaway Inn, is one of the most friendly and outgoing people I've ever known, so it's no surprise that she would want all those close to her to be a part of her big day. As a result, Ella and Javier's wedding party is *big*.

Flora, one of Ella's oldest friends, is serving as her maid of honor, and I'm standing next to Ty, Ella's older brother who just retired from the Army. Ty is serving as Javier's best man. Javier was extremely close with Ty and Ella's dad, George, the former fire chief, so it makes sense Javier would have George's son serve in the spot of honor at his wedding.

Standing to my left is Will, followed by Callum and then Shane, the new chief of the Hideaway Valley police force, having returned to his hometown in December—new wife Noelle in tow. Javier and I have been friends with Shane for years.

Next to Shane is Brodie. Brodie and his wife, Daisy, work for the developer that's building the resort. On their first visit to Hideaway, they were only co-workers staying at the Hideaway Inn on a business trip to check out the property. Their relationship changed after that first visit, and by the time they returned a few months later to start work on the resort, they were married. The two live part-time now in No Name Creek, and have become close friends with us all— Daisy, Flora, Ella, Analise, and Noelle being especially close.

Brodie is flanked by Lucas DeAngelo, the CEO of the

development firm building the resort in Hideaway. Thanks to him, the farmhouse opened its doors early for the wedding. Lucas' wife, Sadie, met Ella a couple of months ago when she first arrived in Hideaway and was staying at the inn. At the time, she was working as Lucas' assistant, but that quickly changed when Lucas found out she was pregnant with his child. The two now live in Hideaway and are building a house near the resort. Sadie has quickly become a member of the lady's close-knit circle, and Lucas is slowly learning how to have friends and a life outside his work.

Now that Ashlyn is back in town, she's been connecting more with all the women and is especially excited to have become friends with Sadie, who is expecting her baby just a few months before our little girl is set to arrive.

Finally, next to Lucas is Beau, Ashlyn's former bodyguard who is now attached to another one of Ella's bridesmaids.

Beau met Briana (the bartender who drove him to the airport when he stayed at the Hideaway Inn) after the fire. Beau came with us to oversee security when we went to London, but when we came back to Hideaway for Christmas he reconnected with Bri and decided to quit his job as a bodyguard to stay with her. Beau and Bri are living together now in Hideaway, where he's working to start a security company—taking everything he learned from what happened to Ashlyn and improving his systems to make them less susceptible to hacking.

Since Ella and Bri became close working together at the inn, she of course had to have Bri in the wedding—which meant Beau was dragged into it as well. The big, stoic man looks slightly out of place, shifting from foot to foot and eyeing the exits. But, just like the rest of us, he'd do anything for his girl. As the other bridesmaids file in, Analise followed by Daisy, Noelle, Sadie, and then finally Bri, Beau's face softens and he nearly smiles.

The only person missing from the wedding, and someone I know is leaving a big hole for Javier especially, is his little sister Gabi. Javier is significantly older than his sister, and although he practically raised her, the siblings are no longer close. When Gabi was in high school she dated Ty, and when he graduated and decided to enlist, they broke up. Gabi blamed Javier for this and insisted on moving to Pueblo to live with extended family for the rest of high school. Gabi recently graduated college and lives in Denver, but despite Ella and Javier's best efforts to get her to attend the wedding, she refused.

I know it isn't easy for Javier not to have Gabi here, but the man is still glowing as Ella starts to make her way down the aisle in a short white dress and a bouquet made of tissue paper and ribbons. Ella is smiling wide as she walks, eyes locked with her fiancé.

I'm so fucking happy for them, knowing first-hand the way it feels to wait for what seems like an eternity before finally finding your person—the one who fills up your heart and soul to overflowing, who makes every single day better, and all the years spent without them completely worth the wait.

Javier takes Ella's hand as she arrives, and they beam at each other as the officiant quickly walks them through what to expect tomorrow.

The officiant concludes his walk-through, and we all take our turns walking back down the aisle and into the adjoining dining room, where we take our seats for dinner.

The evening flies by as we take turns toasting the happy couple and sharing memories about them both until the hour begins to grow late and it's time to head home.

Our hands are clasped and our hearts are full as Ashlyn and I say our goodbyes and head to the parking lot. It's been a great day celebrating love with friends, and I'm certain tomorrow when Javier and Ella make it official, will be even better.

We're settled in the truck and driving home when Ashlyn's phone dings, and then dings again twice more. She pulls it from her purse, tapping to open the message.

"Who is it?" I ask, wondering who would be sending her three texts in a row.

"It's my agent," Ashlyn answers, and I groan.

I like Joan, but the woman just can't seem to understand that Ashlyn isn't taking any new roles right now. Since arriving back in Hideaway, Joan has already reached out twice with offers.

"What is it this time?" I ask.

"It's not about a part," she responds. "It's an article outlining the convictions of my old director. He's been sentenced to twenty years for sexual assault."

"Good," I say. "If you ask me, the fucker got off easy."

She nods. "And it's not just that..." Ashlyn goes on to list the names of several other directors and producers who've just received similar charges. A few were her former *boyfriends;* the men who took advantage of her all those years ago.

I hope they throw the book at them all—lock them up for as long as the law allows.

"I'm so relieved," she says as I pull into our driveway. "I'd already put those men behind me, had already moved on, but now I feel like I can really let my past go. I'm so...so *happy.*" Ashlyn covers my hand where it rests on the center console with her own—face dreamy as she smiles. "Life keeps getting better and better."

I squeeze her hand as I park. "That it does," I say. "And I think I have an idea how we can put the cherry on top of an already perfect day."

Before Ashlyn can get out, I rush to her side of the truck, open the door, and swing her into my arms bridal style.

"Chase!" Ashlyn laughs. "What are you doing?"

"Spending all day practicing for a wedding has inspired me, princess," I say as I carry her inside our cabin.

I offered to sell the place or add on to make the four-bedroom home bigger, but Ashlyn refused. She'd said she was tired of living in mansions and loved how cozy my cabin was, and didn't want to change a thing.

We did, however, need to change the security features. So, I worked with Beau to install cameras and infrared alarm systems all around my two-acre property. Nothing is more important to me than the safety of my growing family.

"Oh yeah?" Ashlyn replies, squealing as I juggle her in my arms, open the front door, and carry her inside.

"Yup," I answer as I rush to our room and throw Ashlyn on the bed. "We may already be married, already had our happily ever after, but I want you just as much now as I did the first time. Tell me you feel the same."

I know she does, but I still like to hear her say it.

"Of course, I do," she says, cupping my face with both hands as I follow her onto the bed, caging her face between my arms. "You know why?"

"Why?" I ask, staring into the most beautiful pair of hazel eyes that have ever existed.

"Because you're the best man I've ever known, Chase Morath. I'll never get enough of you, even after we've been together for years and years and *years*. But right now, at this moment, I'm glad our entire future is still ahead of us. We've got all the time in the world to enjoy each other. I think our happily ever after is just beginning."

I kiss Ashlyn hard and roll her on top of me, holding her tightly to my chest as I trail my lips down the soft column of her neck.

As usual, Ashlyn's right.

I've got my princess in my arms, and our baby is on the way.

Our fairytale is just getting started.

AUTHOR'S NOTE

Thank you for reading *His Hidden Star*! I hope you liked this first book in my new series featuring the firefighters of Hideaway Valley and the women they fall hard and fast for.

If you love romance set in small mountain towns and are curious about the other love stories mentioned in this book, please consider checking out my website or following me on Instagram or Facebook for updates on upcoming releases. Though all the books in the Hideaway universe are interconnected, they can be read as standalone stories.

Before you go, would you also consider leaving me a review? Feedback is crucial for indie authors—especially new ones like me. Thank you in advance!

If you want to read more about Hideaway Mountain (and see how Ashlyn and Chase met) check out my debut novella that started it all—*Hideaway Inn*. As a bonus, I've included the first chapter on the next page!

AUTHOR'S NOTE

Book 2 in Hideaway Valley Fire, *His Hidden Desire*, Ella & Javier's story, is set to release in October of 2024.

Also coming in October is Book 2 in Hideaway Valley Holiday, *Hideaway Halloween*.

EXCERPT: HIDEAWAY INN

CHAPTER ONE: WILL

Social media—*fucking social media* is how I found out that I'd been dumped. Not just dumped, but cheated on, and then dumped.

I was scrolling along on my phone after an exhausting day wrapping my latest film when I came upon a photo from a national entertainment magazine with a picture of my now ex-girlfriend in the arms of the director of her current movie. The headline read simply: "*Ashlyn's New Love?*"

Clicking on the article link, I quickly scanned to find that "…*when asked to comment on the relationship status of the Golden Globe-nominated actress and her hunky romcom star boyfriend, Ashlyn Addison's representatives confirmed that the pair had split.*"

Well—that was news to me.

I can't say I'm heartbroken, exactly, but I am angry and a little hurt. To be honest, I intended on ending things with Ashlyn as soon as she returned from shooting in the U.K., but I at least would have had the decency to talk to her in person.

Instead of calling Ashlyn and taking my frustration out on her though, I decided the moment I read that article I'd had quite enough of Hollywood. The constant real-life drama is about ten times more intense than anything you'd see on screen, and I was so, *so* tired of it. I had to get away.

I called my agent, Tom, and told him—firmly—that I

would not be taking on any new projects for at least a couple of months. As this alone almost gave my usual stoic manager a stroke, I decided I wouldn't yet say anything about the fact that I might be done with acting for good.

It's not like I need the money. I've been one of the most sought-after actors in romantic comedies for the last decade, ever since my debut into the genre at the age of 22, and I'm sick of it.

Sick of playing the same part over and over again.

Sick of reading the insipid scripts sent to me with the most cliché of characters.

What I'd really like to do is write something with substance. Step away from the spotlight, rest, lick my wounds, and write. Ashlyn never would have understood my plan to disappear for a few months.

Despite her distaste for the media gossip, acting is everything to her—another reason why I knew we'd never work out in the long run. Well, that and the fact that we had *zero* sexual chemistry. And now with the public humiliation she's brought upon me, I have the perfect excuse to get away.

So, after calming my frantic agent down, I told him I was going out of town, and asked if he had any recommendations of places I could go that were far from civilization, but not totally off the grid.

I also don't really enjoy being *completely* isolated and alone, so ideally, I told him I would like to stay in a small bed and breakfast or hotel with a few people around. People who hopefully wouldn't recognize me, so I could keep mostly to myself.

The lucky thing about being type-cast is that not everyone is into the niche of movies I appear in, so there is at least a decent chance—with the right concealment, I could manage to go unrecognized.

I just want to hold up for a while in some quiet town with

nice views and good food. I don't need anything fancy. I might be rich and famous now, but that certainly wasn't always the case for me.

"I think I may have just the place," Tom told me after returning from breathing into a paper bag for a few minutes. "I've stayed there when I needed a bit of a reset myself. It's a small inn; a lodge with a few rooms attached to a pub. Decent food and cold beer. Great views. It's in a little Colorado town called Hideaway Mountain."

Hideaway Mountain. The name sounded almost too perfect. "I don't know," I said, holding the phone away on speaker so I could Google the name of the place, "aren't all the mountain towns in Colorado constantly full of tourists?"

I'd gone to Estes Park a few years back in what was supposed to be the offseason, and you could barely drive through the small roads that weren't designed for the number of cars in the street and people on the sidewalks.

"Yeah, but not this one. It's pretty high up in the mountains and isn't near a ski resort or national park. It's tiny too, not much more than a main street with a little general store. They've never even had a movie theatre," he said. "The name of the place I stayed is the Hideaway Inn," he paused and I could hear him typing on his laptop. "It looks like it's still there…oh but lodging looks like it's closed for the season… pub is still open though."

"Closed for the season, in October?" I said, shocked.

It must be a real hole-in-the-wall if they only rent rooms seasonally. I'd made it to the town's less-then high-tech website, and from the few homepage pictures I could tell it was exactly the kind of place I was looking for. A quick search also showed that other than the Hideaway Inn, there weren't any other decent hotels in town.

"It looks like they open again for the holidays in December," Tom said, "but I wonder if they might make an exception for you—for the right price. It's a little family-owned place, the old man who runs it is kind and extremely accommodating. Tell you what, you promise me you'll reset and come back to L.A. before the holiday season so you can do the talk show circuits for the new movie, and I will call and see what I can arrange. Maybe the owner remembers me. I've stayed there several times and always left generous tips," he finished.

I groaned internally in anticipation of the lie I was about to tell Tom—there's no way I'm coming back to do a bunch of talk show interviews after what just happened.

"Sure," I said, "I'll come back to California by the holidays." At least that part wasn't a lie. I can probably commit to that. My mom would kill me if I didn't come home for Christmas, but she lives in San Diego.

"Great," Tom said. "I'll call now and see what I can set up."

So, that's how I ended up here. Standing outside an old log building that looks like it dates back at least a hundred years or more, with my duffel bag across my arm and my other hand gripping the handle of my black suitcase, resting with its wheels on the ground.

I've dyed my normally dark blonde hair black, pulled a Padres baseball cap low on my forehead, and my aviator sunglasses obscure the rest of my face.

I'm also going by my real first name, Will, instead of my screen name, Clarke (my middle name, which, I was told when I started, sounds much more *old-Hollywood,* so would market better). I figure Montgomery is a common enough last name to hopefully fly under the radar, and it's not like I plan to go out and be in any situations where I have to introduce myself anyway.

Tom, miracle worker that he is, was able to sweet talk the new owner—a woman named Flora Wallace, who inherited the place after her grandfather died—into giving me a large room with a kitchenette, on the condition that I clean up after myself since the housekeepers don't work when the lodge portion of the inn is closed.

He also offered to pay a high enough amount for my stay that even *my* eyes bugged out when he told me the price. But, it's not like I can't afford it.

So, after a treacherous drive up the mountains from the airport, I'm finally here. I've arrived at the Hideaway Inn, ready to do exactly that for the next six weeks.

Hide.

TEASER—HIS HIDDEN DESIRE

Ella

Javier Sanchez was my father's best friend. He's also the only man I've ever loved. When my dad died, he made Javier promise to look out for me. Ever since, he's always been there to comfort and protect me—*as friends*. I'm sure his feelings for me run deeper than he'll admit, but he's too honorable to act on them. But I'm tired of waiting for him to make a move, so I join an online dating site. Hideaway Valley is a small community, so I know it's only a matter of time before Javier finds out I have a date with one of the rookies at the fire district. Will I be able to push him over the edge with jealousy, and finally force his hand, or will my plot backfire and push him out of my life for good?

Javier

I've been in love with Ella Monroe since she left college and arrived back in town, but I've always known I can never have her. She's the daughter of the old fire chief and my former mentor, and when he died unexpectedly a few years ago I promised him I'd look out for her. So that's what I've done. But with each passing day and every moment I spend in her presence, it becomes harder and harder for me to fight my urges—*especially* when Ella makes it clear she longs for my touch just as much as I long to touch her. When we finally kiss, the guilt overwhelms me and I tell Ella it can't happen again. Then I find out she has a date with some young punk on my crew, and I don't think I can stand by and let the boy have her. Ella needs a real man to love and protect her, but will I break the promise I made to my best friend?

TEASER—HIDEAWAY HALLOWEEN

Kat

I'm not sure what it is about the old farmhouse in Hideaway Mountain, but I'm determined to save it. The developer I work for, on the other hand, is determined to tear it down. I travel to Colorado prepared to present my case, and when an early season blizzard hits and delays the groundbreaking, I seize my chance. I'm ready to hunker down at the old place on Halloween and spend the storm taking pictures and furthering my plans to incorporate the farmhouse into the new resort. What I'm not prepared for is hunky, businessman Austin Walker—son of the former land owner. He's already there when I arrive, and scares the crap out of me when I discover him in the rundown house. Once Austin tells me why he's there, I can't help but be drawn to him, and begin to wonder if he's the *real* reason I felt so compelled to come here. I'm a good girl though, and determined to keep my distance despite the way he makes my heart flutter. But when we're snowed in together with just one bed and the spooky old house makes me shiver even more than the storm, will I be able to keep resisting the pull between us? Do I even *want* to?

Austin

When I found out my father sold our family's land in Hideaway Mountain without even telling me, I was *furious.* He claims he didn't think I'd want it just because I never wanted to work for his company, which is complete bull. But no matter how mad I am, I can't change the fact that the land was sold, or stop the old farmhouse filled with my happiest memories from being demolished. I need to see it one more time to say goodbye though—so, I take my first-ever vacation from the company I started in California to come back to my hometown. When I arrive, the new owner won't let me on the property, but I've never been one to take no for an answer. I sneak to the farmhouse on Halloween, not anticipating I'd be trapped in a sudden snowstorm with the most *beautiful* woman I've ever seen. Kat Leonard may pretend she doesn't want me, but when we end up huddled together for warmth, I take a chance and steal a kiss—never expecting Kat to retaliate by stealing *my heart.*

WANT A FREE BOOK?

The Grump of Hideaway Mountain, a spicy and sweet novelette featuring a reclusive mountain man and the feisty barista who changes his life, is FREE for my newsletter subscribers! Click here to sign up and get your copy. Already on my list? You can find all my subscriber-exclusive freebies here.

When you join my bimonthly newsletter, you'll have access to more free books and extended epilogues (extended epilogues will be released at the end of 2024), and you'll be the first to hear updates on upcoming books and occasional surprise releases.

Don't want to sign up? That's okay! *The Grump of Hideaway Mountain* is also available to purchase on Amazon.

ALSO BY ELIZA ROCKWOOD

Hideaway Mountain Series:

Novelette: *The Grump of Hideaway Mountain* (Ruby & Hunter's story)

Book 1 (Debut): *Hideaway Inn* (Flora & Will's story)

Book 2: *Hideaway Weekend* (Daisy & Brodie's story)

Book 3: *Hideaway Summer* (Analise & Callum's story)

Book 4: *Hideaway Christmas* (Noelle & Shane's story—Nov 28, 2024: preorder)

Book 5: *Hideaway Boss* (Sadie & Lucas' story—Jan 20, 2025)

Hideaway Valley Fire Series:

Book 1: *His Hidden Star* (Ashlyn & Chase's story)

Book 2: *His Hidden Desire* (Ella & Javier's story—Oct 16, 2024: preorder)

Book 3: *Her Hidden Protector* (Alina & Niko's story—anticipated March 2025)

Book 4: *Her Hidden Hero* (Gabi & Ty's story—anticipated June 2025)

Book 5: *His Hidden Fire* (more info coming soon—anticipated July 2025)

Hideaway Valley Holiday One-Hour Read Series:

Book 1: *Hidden Sparks* (Dani & Hayden's story)

Book 2: *Hideaway Halloween* (Kat & Austin's story—Oct 1, 2024: preorder)

Book 3: *Hideaway New Year* (Briana & Beau's story—Dec 26, 2024)

More holiday stories are coming in late 2024 & early 2025

Next Series: Tempest Knights MC

Coming Spring of 2025

ACKNOWLEDGMENTS

Thanks as always to my husband, for being patient through the hours and hours I spend writing, editing my first books, and using his artistic talents to create my book covers.

Thanks to my friend Kate, for being the first person to ever read one of my books, encouraging me to publish, and serving as an occasional proofreader.

Thanks to my author friend August Lindsay for sharing this new indie author journey with me, and for responding to my random messages for advice whenever I find myself stuck.

For this book in particular, thanks to Natalie for taking on the role of my first-ever beta reader, and for helping me start a Street Team. If you're looking for some great reading recommendations, give her a follow on Instagram. I promise you won't be disappointed: @natalies_world_in_books.

And finally, thanks to my ARC and Street Team for reading, reviewing, and hyping up my books. Y'all are the absolute best! <3

ABOUT THE AUTHOR

Eliza lives in Denver, Colorado with her husband and two dogs. When she's not writing, she can be found reading, hiking, doing yoga, or at her "real job" as a political science professor. Though the *Hideaway Mountain* series is her debut published work, Eliza has been writing since she was a kid (was even presented with the esteemed *"Future Novelist"* award in her fifth-grade class), and has an undergraduate degree in creative writing. She is happy to finally be realizing a lifelong dream of publishing her written work.

If you'd like to connect with Eliza, check out her website at elizarockwood.com or send her a message on Instagram (@author_elizarockwood) Threads, or Facebook.

Printed in Great Britain
by Amazon